Princesses of the Pizza Parlor

by Maikel Yarimizu

To the one and only Helen, from her Uncle.

Table of Contents

Episode 1

"Princesses Don't Do Summer School"

Max's Pizza wasn't the biggest restaurant in town, or the busiest, or even the tastiest — though lots of people said it was anyway. The building had once been a burger joint, and then an ice cream parlor, but Max had done such a number on the place that you'd never know unless you'd lived here all your life. Red-checked cloth covered the tables, and there was a counter along the far end where you could pick up a slice of whatever was available. If you wanted something else, Max was usually happy to oblige.

There were corner booths with deep old sofa seats, leather worn and cracked, and broad tables that were useful for so many things. A lot of business meetings happened here during the week.

It was Sunday afternoon, though, right after the lunch rush brought in all the families after church. One table was wiped clean of crumbs, and now had all sorts of things gathered upon it.

A white laptop computer, not too old and not too new, sat to the side. A pile of colorful books lay next to it, and tons of loose paper. A cardboard box was filled with little figurines, no two alike. And in a big old Mason jar, there were dice, more dice than a kid might think existed. Some were square, with six sides, but more were not. There were little plastic pyramids that counted only to four, and others with so many sides that they were almost round. Those counted up to twenty. There was even a blue one that really was round, and it rattled when you shook it.

Helen let the little blue ball fall from her hands and watched it roll across the table. It stopped right in the middle, showing six white dots in two rows.

"If you're gonna mess with the dice, be useful and get them sorted for everyone," her uncle said. He turned back to his conversation. "Thanks again for letting us set up here, Maxine."

"Not a problem. Sunday afternoon and evening are always pretty slow for walk-ins, anyway. And it's Max. You know that." The owner and operator of Max's Pizza was dressed in her usual black slacks, white shirt, and red vest. She looked real smart in it, especially when she stood next to Uncle in his faded jeans and flannel.

The dice came in a crazy rainbow of colors, but it was easy enough to sort them into crowds of sorta-red, kinda-blue, mostly orange, probably purple, and greenish. All the rest — the clears, the blacks, the metallics, and the whatevers — she piled up behind the divider screen at Uncle's seat.

"So when are your little friends arriving?" Max picked up a couple of sparkly red dice and rattled them in her fist. "The pies will take a while to cook, after all. Pepperoni still good?"

"And a small supreme for me," said Uncle as he arranged his papers.

"Yes, please," Helen said. "Are you sure you don't want to play too?"

"Sweetie, I haven't had the time to sit down for a game in years. I'll just let you and friends have your fun, and I'll enjoy from the counter."

Helen scooted to her place in the middle of the wide sofa seat and organized her greenish dice in neat lines according to size. First the twenties, then the twelves, the tens, the eights, the sixes, and then her one little four-sided die, a light green with swirls of yellow. She rolled it once, just to see, and it came out with a 3 on its top point.

"Here's your character sheet, kiddo." Uncle slid the paper over. "Got everything we talked about."

"Thanks, Uncle!"

"Still can't believe your niece talked you into this," said Max.

"What can I say? She saw it on TV, wanted to give it a go, and I'm the only one in the family who knows anything about it. Oh, Helen. Is that one of yours?" He pointed out the window to a blue sedan that had just parked on the side. Two girls were hopping out. One was skinny and taller with a thick mane of orange-brown hair pulled back into a ponytail. The other girl was a full head shorter, with brown pigtails and bangs that almost completely hid her eyes from view. Both of them had enough freckles each to form their own constellations.

"Cynthia! Katelyn!" Helen called and banged on the window until she'd caught the girls' attention. She ran to the door and greeted them with hugs and squeals.

Uncle had resigned himself to a long afternoon, but he put on a good face and shook Mr. McAll's hand. The man had the look of a dad who was already wishing summer vacation was over, and all he'd done was ferry his daughter and her friend to a playdate.

"Thanks for doin' this," Cynthia's father mumbled through his moustache. "The girls seem t' be lookin' forward to it."

"Yeah, they do. And thanks for chipping in for the pizza and all."

"Worth it, young man. Worth it." And with that, the dad beat a hasty retreat.

"So!" Uncle said, turning back to the table. "We're just missing two, right?"

"Nope, just one," came a voice from right beside his elbow. Uncle jumped, tripped, and nearly fell over a roll on the carpet.

"Claire!" cried Helen. "When'd you get here?"

"Just now. Rode my bike in." The tiny girl waddled over to the table, then climbed up onto a seat. Her legs didn't quite reach the floor, and her thick, round spectacles barely made it above the table's edge. A single oversized bow stuck out from the back of her dark brown hair like a pair of floppy rabbit ears.

"Okay then," said Uncle. "Who's missing?"

"Just Shelby," his niece said. She and the other girls piled onto the old sofa seat. "Not sure if she's coming. She wasn't really into the idea."

"I guess we can start then, and she can

catch up when she gets here." Uncle picked up a sheaf of paper and tapped it even. Each page had a logo on it, plus a bunch of lines and a whole bunch of numbers. "So, everyone knows what we're up to today?"

"We're gonna have an adventure!" shouted Cynthia.

"Gonna tell a story!" Helen added.

"...be princesses," Katelyn mumbled, her eyes darting back and forth a little nervously from behind her bangs.

"More or less all of that. Including the last one." Uncle didn't quite groan at that, but he really wanted to. That had been one of the few things that was completely non-negotiable with his niece. If they were playing a fantasy story game, then there had to be princesses. And since she didn't want her friends to feel left out, they could all be princesses, too. He'd just done his best to accommodate. "So in this game, you each get a character that you have to role-play. She can be just like you, or a completely different person. It's your choice, and you'll have some time right here at the start to change things up or choose how she looks. Anything you want, but," he added with a tap on the paper, "she's completely defined by what's on her sheet here. You can't decide a few hours in that she knows kung-fu or anything, just because it's convenient. So we're going to work on who we are, first of all. Helen, why don't you introduce them to your princess, since we already worked her details out?"

"Okay, Uncle! Ahem, my princess is named Gwenevrael, and she's..."

Gwenevrael sat on her favorite branch of her favorite tree in her favorite part of the woods surrounding Lady Amberyll's Academy for Young Ladies. She had her special cloak out, the one her father had given her as a parting gift before she'd left for school, and the magic woven into it made her extra hard to see against the bark.

This came in extra handy when she wanted to hunt, but she wasn't hunting today. Gwenevrael liked to sit here and think sometimes, and pretend there was no one else around for miles but rabbits and squirrels and deer and hawks. Sometimes her lightly pointed ears caught the sound of a deer passing by. Sometimes she'd imagine it was a unicorn, even though she knew better.

Eventually she grew tired of hiding and

flipped back the hood of her cloak to reveal the pale skin and arrow-tipped ears of her father's family matched with her mother's red hair and freckles. The sky-blue eyes were hers alone.

She jumped to the ground, startling a family of rabbits as she did, and started walking back to the Academy.

"... so her sheet tells us at the top that Gwen here is a half-elf, and that she's trained as a ranger."

"That anythin' like a forest ranger?" asked Cynthia.

"Sort of, but with more arrows and magic. Now, these numbers here along the top are for things like how strong she is, how fast, how smart, stuff like that. Whenever Helen wants her to do something difficult, these are the numbers we'll be checking. For example, she's got a high dexterity — she's fast and good with her hands," he added quickly. "So, any time she has to do something quick and tricky, she gets a plus-three bonus. With me so far?"

"What's the stuff along the side?" asked

Claire. The little girl was standing on her seat to look at the paper better. "Hm... Riding, climbing, swimming..."

"Just what it looks like," said Uncle. "Those are things that she is, or can be, good at, with the bonuses based on the numbers up top. Now, I've already drawn up a bunch of characters with their base stats and skills assigned, so we could get things started faster. What kind of princess would you like to be?"

"Like Snow White!" hollered Cynthia. "Y'know, singin' and happy and gettin' animals to like her and all."

"Druid princess it is! That means you get to use nature magic and you have an animal companion," he explained as he handed her the paper. "And for you other young ladies?"

"...um.. could... could I..." Katelyn mumbled. "Can witches be princesses?"

"She's always a witch. Every Halloween." Helen rolled her eyes, and Katelyn's blush spread out from under those brown bangs.

"Nothing wrong with that. And yes, I've got a witch princess in here. Glad I drew some from outside the core classes now. Here you are." He passed the sheet over. "Okay, how about you, C—"

"I am the moon princess, here to fight for love and justice and happiness and the future of the Moon Kingdom!" The girl stood on her tiptoes and brandished a plastic wand with a red crystal held in a crescent moon shape. "And I'm tall and beautiful and strong and all the evil monsters of the dark dimensions shall fear me!"

"Tall?" snorted Cynthia.

"Now, now, I already said that your princess does not have to be just like you. So, Claire. You like those Japanese cartoons, I take it?"

"Yeah! Wanna know which one's my favorite?"

"I think I can guess," said Uncle. "Let me check what I've got on my laptop..." Tap-tap-click. "Okay, you can be a cleric princess. That means you're a holy girl who gets her magic from a god or goddess. There isn't an official Moon goddess in the system we're using, but we can always make one up. Okay!" Uncle announced as he pulled a stack of index cards from his bag. "Three of you are able to use magic, so we need to go over some basics. First, Helen, could you get the bag of flat marbles? Give everyone else three blues each. For the reds, Katelyn and Claire get two, and Cynthia gets one."

"What're these s'posed to be?" the pony-tailed girl asked. "Looks like somethin' from the bottom of a goldfish bowl."

"These represent your magic spells," Uncle explained. He picked up a blue. "These are for level one spells, which your characters should know a few of, and the reds are for level two spells, of which they know exactly one each. I already filled out the list on the back of your sheet for you, but we can change them up a little if you want."

He showed them the index cards, which had colored tabs in green, blue, or red. "These have the details of each spell written on them. Green ones are the so-called level zero spells, which do a bunch of useful but boring things like fetching, cleaning, or mending. You get to choose four of these each day, but you can use them any way you want, as much as you want."

Helen took the cards and the other girls crowded around to check them out. It had taken Uncle most of an afternoon and evening to fill out the necessary information in a way that was clear, and he'd tried to make it funny as well, with descriptions like "Makes a magic snowball that you can stuff in someone's ear, down their pants, wherever. Good for getting people to chill out." He hoped their giggles were for the jokes he'd actually intended.

This gave him free moment to check over some details, at least. Silently, he thanked Max for giving him the shop's wi-fi key. Having an internet connection available made things so much easier. "Okay, Claire? Could you come over for a bit?"

"Yes, o inimitable maestro of the grand game of the imagination?"

"... save it for the roleplay, kid." He pulled a chair over so she could see the laptop screen with him. "So a cle... er, holy girl's got to choose some things called domains. Has to do with who they're supposed to be serving, and how that deity influences the world. I'm guessing you're okay with the Love and Moon domains?"

"In the name of the Moon, I shall bring peace and love to the world!"

"Right... I'll take that as a yes. Now, as a holy girl —"

"Princess."

"Yes, as a holy princess, you get a few extra tricks connected to your domain. On top of that, I can give your holy scepter a special power based on the Moon..." He scribbled a note and handed it to her to read.

"Um.. does this say I get a light saber?"

"I guess you could call it that. You can only use it a limited amount of time per day," he added. "Based on your character's level."

"Awesome. Um, what level are we starting at? One?"

"Good question. Okay, ladies!" he called for attention. "Seeing as you are all princesses, Helen and I came to some agreements. First, you're all starting at level three, probably because of excellent tutoring options."

"Awesomesauce! Moon Laser Sword Magic!"

"Um, Mr. Man?" Cynthia raised her hand. "How do we get magic back after we use it?"

"That depends. You all need to get a good night's sleep to really recharge, but beyond that, druids need to meditate on nature for a bit. Moon Princesses need to say their prayers every evening. Witches just need a good rest and some quality time with their familiars. Now, have you all cho—"

"NO, NO, NO! I don't wanna and you can't make me!"

All heads turned to the front door, where a tanned, burly man with with more blond hair on his face than on his head was all but carrying a girl one-handed into the restaurant. This was a particularly impressive feat because she was taller than any of the kids at the table by almost a full head, and looked like she spent most of her time running around outside and kicking stuff.

"Now, now!" said her father. "You promised your friends you'd be here, and I ain't gonna let you weasel out of it that easily. See? They're already here!"

"Hi, Shelby!" shouted Helen, with the chorus of other girls following a moment later.

"Hrmph." The girl managed to slouch her way across the room, squeezing onto the couch next to the others.

"I'll be back to pick you up around six, honey!"

"Whatever." Shelby's face was so sour it could be mistaken for lemonade. Curly black hair stuck out in all directions, but mostly downward to the collar of her soccer team t-shirt.

"So, er, Shelby," said Uncle. "Ready to be a princess?"

"No."

"Aw, don't be like that," said Helen. "It's not going to be dresses and balls and stuff. We're going to have adventures!"

"Defend nature!" cried Cynthia.

"...do magic stuff."

"Punish evil-doers in the name of the Moon!"

"Anything you want, really," said Uncle. "Helen, how about you go over the options with her? We could use a fighter of some sort in this game."

That perked up Shelby a little. "So I don't gotta be some stupid Disney pretty princess?"

"Well, I made it a house rule that everyone's got the same charisma score, so you're all equally pretty princesses, but..." Uncle shrugged. "It's your show, ladies. I'm just organizing this madhouse. If you want to change your characters, customize them a bit, then now is the time."

"C'mon, Shelby. Let's get you a cool battle princess," said Helen. She grabbed the remaining character sheets, as well as a couple old art books that Uncle had brought along.

"Good, good. Now, um, Katelyn? Could you come over?"

"...yes?"

"You'll need to speak a little louder, kid. First question, what sort of familiar animal do you want for your witch?"

"... can I have a cat?"

"Excuse me?"

"I..." The girl coughed, then raised her voice a little. "Can I have a little black cat with a white spot on his chest?"

"Don't see why not. And kitties give you a bonus on stealth, so..." He checked a few boxes on her character sheet. "You're all set for some sneaky shenanigans. That okay with you?"

His only answer was a shy smile.

"Okay, now as a witch, you can get some special tricks. I've got the list here somewhere..." He pawed through a ringed notebook for a second. "Yeah, here we are. Hexes. Choose two."

Katelyn squinted through her bangs at the scribbled notes. Uncle's handwriting was if anything worse than the fifth-grade average, but he'd tried to keep it readable. Quietly, she picked out two tricks from the list and wrote them on her sheet.

"Interesting selections. This should be fun."

"Could I please have these spells for my princess, pleeeeeeeeeeeeze?" Cynthia crashed in from the side, shoving a piece of paper in Uncle's face. Her handwriting was about as messy as his, only written larger and with kitty paw prints above the i's and j's.

"Um... Summon Animal, Summon Nature's Allies, Converse with Animals..." He continued reading. "Er, Cynthia, do all of these have to do with animals?"

"Yup!" The girl bounced on her seat, sending her ponytail up and down.

"Okay, some of these are redundant, and a couple are completely out of your ability level. This last one... All-Out Animal Apocalypse is not a real spell, so no."

"Awww...."

"Palaver time!" Uncle called. "Claire, get back over here! We're working on spell lists."

It didn't take that long to sort everything out, though he'd had to put his foot down a few times before they had any sort of agreement. He needed to resign himself to the fact that none of the girls made the sort of decisions he would, but then again, wasn't that the point?

"We're ready!" announced Helen from the other side of the table. She and Shelby had a character sheet in front of them, covered in fresh pencil smudges and eraser boogies.

"Really?" said Uncle. "That was fast. Okay then, tell us what you've got."

Shelby squared her shoulders, picked up the character sheet, and began. "Princess Selvi..."

Princess Selvi, youngest daughter of the Grand Khan of the high plains of Dungivadim, was in the middle of her second morning practice. The first had been a warm-up, an easy hour to stretch her arms and legs and listen to the blade of her scimitar sing as it flew through the air. After a half-hour break and a lot of water, she did it all over again, only in full armor this time. Sweat covered her forehead as she cut through the air, but her beloved drake-scale armor was so wonderful, it moved with her, no problem. Her illustrious father, may his name ever be feared, had given it to her himself before she'd left to attend this stinking school for soft, weak little girls.

Well, she wasn't about to let this place get to her. She was Selvi Khan's-daughter, strong and hot as the desert wind, and she would fight all challengers.

Her practice came to an end in front of a large glass mirror, which was there mainly for the other princesses' dance lessons later in the day. It was bigger and finer than any of the brass mirrors back home, and it was perfect for watching herself move. Taking off her helmet with its horse-hair crest, she shook her own blue-black braids. She wiped the sweat from her face, dark and dusky like her mother's, but with the greenish color of her honored father's people. A wild grin crossed her face, showing two delicate tusks.

The clan leaders back home looked down on her for her mixed blood, but the girls here feared her for it. Selvi knew which feeling she liked more. One day she would return to the hills of Dungivadim and make sure everyone there felt the same way.

"A half-orc barbarian?" Uncle sounded like he didn't believe what his ears were telling him.

"A half-orc barbarian *princess*," Shelby

corrected. She'd borrowed a hair clip from Helen, so all that curly black hair was pulled back from her face now. "Strong, tough, and plays soccer with the heads of her enemies. You got a problem with that?" The girl stuck out her lower lip and flared her nostrils, daring him to say he did.

"Nope. Anyone else? Helen?" Uncle asked, looking at his niece's character sheet. He knew for a fact that it had 'Enemy of all orcs' written somewhere on it.

"Sounds cool!" "... no problem." "We shall defend the righteous together!" came the chorus from his side of the table.

"Gotta make things interesting. Right, Uncle?" Helen said with a wink.

"Alright then, it sounds like you two have plenty to roleplay over. So!" he continued. "One last thing before our magic-users introduce themselves. I noticed Shelby made special mention of her armor, and earlier on Helen's princess had a magic cloak. That stuff's not standard for beginning adventurers. You all are princesses, so I'm allowing you each two heirloom items that are a lot nicer than your characters should have right now. FYI," he added. "If a monster's shooting fire at you, hide behind Princess Selvi."

He opened his ringed notebook to one last

list. This one had been decorated in gold pen by Helen the other day, and had shiny curlicues all around the edges. "You each have one item already on your sheets, but there's space for another. Anything on here is okay."

"I picked a magic arrow-holder thing," Helen added.

"A quiver."

"Yeah, that was it. Thanks, Uncle. It never runs out of arrows."

Uncle had been more than happy to let her have that one, too. There were already enough things to pay attention to that he didn't want to add keeping track of arrows in a big fight. The rest of the list was eclectic, filled with items that were obviously useful as well as a few that were just plain silly. As the girls bickered over what to choose, he allowed himself a quick grin.

"Ooh! A lute!" shouted Cynthia, stabbing a finger at the paper. "That's like a guitar, right?"

"Um, sort of."

"Awright! Gonna get that," the pony-tailed girl declared. "And I'm gonna sing all the animals to do what I want 'em to do."

"Er, you do realize your character has no

skill points in performance, right?" he asked, while everyone else around the table groaned and shook their heads.

Neither reaction seemed to discourage the girl at all, if she even noticed. Instead, she sat up in her seat and started to sing: "*Oh, since my puppy left me... I been all over town...* " Uncle couldn't tell if what came next was improvised, or if there really was a rockabilly song out there about runaway pets, but Cynthia was really belting it out, as enthusiastic as she was off-key.

"Hey, game guy," Claire said, once the song was over.

"Just call him Uncle," Helen said with a giggle.

"Okay, Uncle game guy! Is this mythril stuff the same magic silver from those movies with the elves and the ring and stuff?"

"Er, yes. It's sometimes called moon silver, too..."

"Perfect! I'm grabbing this mythril chain vest then. Moon Princess Protection!" The little girl was standing on her seat again, waving her plastic scepter wildly.

Her Holy Highness Princess Cassandrella, the next High Priestess of the Moon Throne of Selunika, stretched her long legs and then knelt on her prayer cushion. She was on the dormitory's roof, in a flat little space reserved especially for her, because her work was so important. Someone had to greet the Moon every day as it rose over the horizon, which according to her little schedule book would happen in the late afternoon today. It didn't necessarily have to be her doing it, of course. Her blessed mother was certainly making her prayers right now as well, but every little bit helped.

There! That beautiful half-circle, light of her life, peeked over the mountains to the east. Cassandrella raised her scepter of office, sign of her service as priestess of the Moon, and saluted. The sleek mythril baton was topped by a shimmering crystal caught in a crescent of pale gold.

"I greet thee today, O Bounteous Moon, bringer of light in the darkness, wife of the Sun! To Thee do we cry when misfortune strikes in the night, and from Thee do we gain the strength to strike back. Let me bear Thy gift, O Moon, and be Thy righteous light!"

Pretty much every day, she asked the Moon to accept her service, and every night, the Moon said yes. She could feel the blessings of Her power flowing down, making her holy symbol shine with the light of love.

Princess Cassandrella stood tall and, clad in her moon-silk robes and fuzzy bunny slippers, she danced to the light of the Moon in the pale blue sky.

"Claire? Claire!" Uncle was calling. "Earth to Moon Princess, come in!"

Brown eyes opened wide, made even larger by the huge bottle frame lenses on her face. Everyone was staring at her attempts to pirouette on the old sofa seat. Her ankles wobbled, and she fell right onto Shelby.

"Hey! Watch whatcher doin', ya little baby!"

"Who're you calling little?" Claire yelled back before she could sit properly. "We're all the same age!"

"Barely."   Shelby snorted.   "You turned twelve in, what, May? And I'm turning thirteen in August."

"So we're in a three-month window of opportunity?   Great!" Uncle declared loudly, clapping his hands. "What will your princess take, Shelby?"

"Whatever."

"Okay then, bone talisman! Carved from a dragon's knuckle," he added.   "Perfect for barbarian princesses or heavy metal aficionados. Okay, last up is Katelyn. Have you picked anything out yet?"

"...There's no magic broomstick."

"Um, I didn't quite catch that."

"She said there's no magic broomsticks," reported Helen. "Y'know, like for flying."

Uncle shrugged.   "Sorry, but I wanted to keep the items on the list at or around the same price, by the game rules. A magic broom of flying would cost at least five times what anything else would be, and your witch's already got a pretty awesome item on her sheet."

"Awww..." said Claire. "Let her have it..."

"Yeah, c'mon," chimed in Cynthia.

"It's not that... Look," said Uncle. He shook his head. "This would give her a steed, a flying one, and the rest of you don't even have horses! It's not a good idea for game balance, or... or..."

Five pairs of puppy-dog eyes stared at him from around the table. Katelyn even had her hand pulling her bangs up just to get the effect right. In ragged unison, the girls all cried, "Pleeeeeeeeeze?"

"Fine. Fine!" Uncle threw his hands up on the air. "What do I know? I'm just the GM here. Okay! So, Princess... what was her name?"

"... Bianca."

"Bianca, Uncle."

"Princess Bianca **had** a magic broom, a really nice one made of sanded elm wood with a leather seat and everything, only there was an incident a couple of weeks ago involving some silly game with enchanted, weighted balls, and a fellow princess got sent to the infirmary with a concussion, so the broom's currently locked in a closet in the teachers' lounge. Hey," he said to his audience. "I never said I'd make it easy on you all. Now, Cynthia. It's time to introduce your character."

"Awright!" Her reddish ponytail bounced as the girl played air-lute for a moment, then began: "This is the ballad of Flora the Fair..."

This is the ballad of Flora the Fair...
With rosy-red cheeks and golden hair...
Like waves of grain upon the plain...
And a voice like birdsong in the air...

A fingernail caught on a lute string, pulling it with a loud twang and a muffled curse. Princess Flora Fidella Del'Monica sucked her finger until the pain subsided, and then started over. Writing a song was harder than it sounded, though. She'd already run out of good rhymes for "fair". Flair? Pair? Pear? Spare?? Nothing really fit.

She sighed. "Got any ideas, Mr. Chitters?"

Up above, from his perch atop Flora's Staff of Plenty, Mr. Chitters the squirrel twitched his red tail and squeaked some advice in a quick burst of clicks and chirps. Squirrel poetry left a lot to be desired, unfortunately. Everything seemed to rhyme with "nuts".

"Welp, it's getting late," she said, noting the sun's place in the sky. "Better be getting back to the Academy."

Mr. Chitters squeaked in protest.

"Yah, yah. I don't like it much either, but at least they let us spend the afternoons out here, right?" In between the school's keep and the outer walls, there was a nice-sized wood that was filled with all sorts of cute and cuddly critters. Only Mr. Chitters ever came back with her to school, though, and that was 'cause he was her special companion. He'd come with her all the way from the forested slopes of Silvalachia, and would sometimes complain about the local squirrels' funny accent.

Flora uprooted her Staff of Plenty from where she had planted it in the ground. It'd been her grandfather's, and she was always amazed at how the roots and branches pulled back into it and became patterns in the carved wood whenever it wasn't planted right. There hadn't been enough time this afternoon for it to grow fruit, though her mouth watered at the thought.

The druid princess waved to all the other animals, the birds and the rabbits and the deer that had come to hear her sing. Her audience scattered and disappeared into the brush. With a sigh, she turned and headed back to school.

"Not bad, Cynthia." Uncle nodded. "You read the notes on your character sheet, too. Any questions?"

"Is the lute magic, too?" The girl looked like she was about to break out in song again.

"Yes, but I'm not going to tell you how just yet." Uncle winked. "Gotta have some surprises. So let's get this game started for real, shall we? It's the last day of school, and..."

"Uncle!" yelled Helen. "You forgot to let Katelyn introduce her character!"

"What? Oh, sorry about that." He brought his palms together and made a polite sort of bow in her direction. "My apologies. So, tell us about Bianca."

"...Princess Bianca."

Princess Bianca of the Western Winkwoods was buried in books. They were piled high on all sides, leaning in precariously but never actually toppling over. She had her own nest of cushions in the heart of the pile, and she was curled up with a huge tome, an index of magic items. At her side was a large rod, or perhaps a scepter, fancy and ornate with gold wire and gemstone chips. It was a gift from her grandmother, the Witch of the Winkwoods, and it looked quite impressive. She just didn't know what it actually did.

It was up to her to figure it out, she'd been told. One more riddle from Gran'Mama, the old bat. The teachers here at the Academy wouldn't let her test it out directly, either — not until she knew what it was supposed to do. So ever since her broom had gotten impounded over that stupid ball game accident, she'd stuck to the library with its huge selection of magical encyclopediae and indices. The answer had to be in there somewhere!

Her hat, big and floppy brimmed like a witch's should be, was scrunched up between a set of bookends. Her familiar uncurled his body from around the pointy end and meowed softly. Jinkies was a cute little black cat with a white star on his chest and a huge appetite hiding behind it. He considered it his duty to make sure she was alerted to all mealtimes promptly and with great protest.

"Mrrow! Mrrgl?" Jinkies hopped up on her

shoulder and began licking her ear.

"Okay, okay! I'll take a break for lunch!" She placed her bookmark carefully, set the index to the side, and picked up her hat and scepter. "Come along, Jinkies."

The little cat took his habitual place around her collar as she left her fortress of solitude and study. The way the books were stacked, there was no way to go but up, which didn't trouble her at all. Bianca ran a hand through her black hair, picking out the single lock of pure white that hung down the front of her face. There was a trick her grandmother had taught her, a way to focus a bit of her magic through that lock of hair and make it stretch, extend, and reach up, up, up out of the pile. The rest of her followed right after, pulled up by that magic hair.

She held on to her treasure tightly. It was a mystery and a challenge, and she wouldn't stop until she knew the answer. She would succeed. She knew she would!

"... And I'll find out what it does! For real!..." Katelyn's voice tapered off as she realized she'd just been shouting at the table. Then Uncle began clapping, and a blush flared across her face like a wildfire. She sat back down and tried to disappear into the crevices of the sofa seat.

"No, no, no! That was good!" cried Helen, pulling the other girl back up.

"That it was," Uncle agreed. "Good to hear your voice, kid."

The blush didn't fade, but it was joined by the girl's shy smile.

"Breadsticks coming through!" Max swooped in with a basket of appetizers. "You all were looking a little hungry over here. When's a good time to get the pizzas ready?"

"In about an hour?" Uncle suggested. "We're about to take the princesses out for a test drive. Girls! Get your drinks now, or be thirsty for a while longer. Your choice."

The pizza parlor had a self-service drink counter by the register, and while the young ladies were debating the selection, he took the opportunity to re-order the table. When they returned with their drinks and his requested root beer, it was to find a laminated map of a castle that — in this particular game — was known as Lady Amberyll's Academy for Young Ladies. The last time he'd pulled it out of storage, it had been the lair of an undead king, but with a bit of dry erase marker and some new sticky labels it had quickly been transformed. Around the map, each girl's character sheet was neatly placed along with whatever reference cards and magic counters were needed.

In the center of the map were six figurines. Five had once been chess pawns, but they'd gotten a paint job and a sort of promotion somewhere along the way. The sixth figure was very much still a queen.

"There'll be a little color sticker on the corner of your sheet," said Uncle. "Your princess is a matching color. So on to business! It's the last day of school for the summer, and all the princesses are packed and ready to go through the magic Wayhouse doors to their homelands. You ladies are in the last group to go, but before you can leave, the headmistress summons you to her office...."

Lady Amberyll's office was lofty and classically decorated, much like its mistress. Even when seated in her chair, she towered over the five girls. Her hair was silver, but otherwise she did not look old at all. Sharp green eyes watched the princesses as they filed in, and the ghost of a smile slid across her face.

"Good morning, children," she said.

"Good morning, milady," they responded in chorus, though Princess Selvi rolled her eyes as she joined in.

"Now, I know you must all be busy with the end of the school year," Lady Amberyll continued. "But I have some unfortunate news. The five of you all pass through the Alford Point Wayhouse on the way to your respective realms every holiday, but unfortunately that house was attacked just last night. Stone trolls, you know, very messy things. The magic door was completely knocked to pieces, I'm afraid."

She paused for a moment, watching as they digested this bit of news. The young half-elf caught on the quickest, raising her hand politely.

"Yes, Gwenevrael?"

"What, or rather, how does this affect our travel plans?"

"It rather ruins them. While it may be possible to arrange passage through other

Wayhouses, there would by necessity be some long overland trips between them. None of you would likely reach home before it was time to turn around and return here. We are preparing message spells to inform your respective courts of the issue, and that you are free to stay on school grounds for the summer."

The young ladies all reacted to that, though some more than others. Gwenevrael simply frowned and looked sad, while Bianca seemed almost happy. Flora and Cassandrella were on the verge of tears, but dear, sweet Selvi...

"This stinks like camel slop!"

... was her usual, charming self.

"Language, Selvi," Lady Amberyll tutted. "Now, I know this is a bit sudden, but at least you're not alone. I'm sure the five of you will find something in common."

The headmistress did have to admit that this was something of a long-shot, though. Already the half-elf was glaring daggers at the khan's daughter, with young Cassandrella sitting uneasily between them. The three were as mismatched a set as any she'd seen, with the ranger's greens, the barbarian's dark red and black, and the moon princess's shimmery white raiment all together like that. And then there was Flora on the far left, in homespun cotton and simple leather, not looking a bit like a lady of high birth. On the far right, Bianca had her usual black gown on, as well as that ridiculously large hat she insisted on wearing everywhere.

And then the young witch's cat, who'd spent the last few minutes quietly stalking the druid's squirrel, chose that moment to pounce.

"Mrrowl!" "Squeak!" "Mr. Chitters!" "Hey! Watch where you're—" "Get off me!" "In the name of the Moon—!" "If you touch Jinkies, I'll..."

"Enough!" Lady Amberyll roared, forcing all five girls and two pets into silence. "Like it or not, the five of you will be stuck together for the rest of the summer." The headmistress nailed each of them in turn with her sternest glare. "I understand how disappointed you all must be, but you need to live with it. Now, I would suggest that the five of you retire to the parlor on your floor and get to know each other better. Perhaps plan what you would like to do for the holidays."

A moment later, and they were standing in the cool stone hall of the Academy, with the headmistress's door clicking shut behind them. Ten minutes later, they were sitting around a table in the parlor, just as Lady Amberyll had commanded.

Flora was handing out cups of her favorite herbal tea, the one made with raspberries. Only Selvi turned down the offer. The barbarian princess was slouching back in an overstuffed armchair. Across the table from her, Gwenevrael was carefully cleaning her knives, but accepted her cup with one thin-gloved hand. Bianca was sitting on the rug, her cat perched atop her shoulder.

Cassandrella was running into the room with her hands full of clean bed sheets.

"What are you going on about?" Selvi growled.

"I heard this in a story! You cut the linens into strips and make a rope so you can climb down from your bedroom window and escape!"

"We're not confined to our rooms," Gwenevrael pointed out. The ranger princess aimed a thumb at her pack, laid out on the floor beside her. "And some of us actually have rope."

"Oh..." The cleric dumped the linens on the floor, then sat on them with a *whoomph*. "Oh! We could make a big balloon out of them and fly right over the walls! Bianca could pull us with her broom!"

Uncle scribbled a quick note and passed it over to Katelyn.

"... oh."

"What does it say?" asked Helen.

"Flying's not such a good idea," Bianca said, hugging Jinkies. "I tried to fly over the walls once. The gargoyles almost ate me." She shivered at the memory and squeezed tightly. The little black cat rolled his eyes and mewled.

"Where would we even go?" asked Flora.

"Anywhere but here," Selvi said. "Spent enough time here as it is. Ain't staying any longer."

"Let's go to the Moon!" Everyone ignored Cassandrella this time.

"Has anyone even been out the main gates before?" asked Bianca. The other girls shook their heads. Like all the princesses at the school, they'd always arrived by Wayhouse, and left the same way.

"Surely one of us knows where we could go!"

"Okay, time out," said Uncle. "This is the perfect opportunity for a knowledge check. The idea is that just because you don't know something doesn't mean your princess doesn't know it, if you get my drift. So for example, Gwen's got a skill point in knowledge of geography. With her other scores and everything, she's got a good chance of knowing where to go. Ready, Helen?"

His niece grinned and picked up her big green die, the one with numbers up to twenty.

"So, the difficulty here is fifteen for full knowledge, but you've got a bonus of seven already. Eight or higher gets it."

The little lump of green plastic rolled from her fingertips, landing on the tabletop and bouncing once, twice, three times. *Gatta-gatta-gatta...* The die came up with a 3. Helen stared at the number for a moment, then looked to her uncle with a confused face. "Um, what do we do now?" she asked.

"We roll with it. Here's what a total of ten gets you..."

"The Academy's out in the middle of nowhere on purpose," Gwenevrael said with a sigh. "That's why everyone uses the Wayhouses to get here. I'm not even sure where we'd be on a map."

"So why don't we find one? A map, I mean." Everyone turned to look at Bianca, still sitting cross-legged on the soft carpet. "We've got a library over in the next building, and it's not like they said we couldn't use it for study purposes."

"But will the librarian let us see the right books?" asked Selvi. "She never lets me touch anything."

"Probably she was convinced you'd rip all the pages," snorted Gwenevrael.

"I prefer ripping ears. Pointy ones make for good handholds, too."

"May the Moon bring peace!" shouted Cassandrella, pushing herself between them. "We'll be stuck here all summer at this rate, unless we can work together at least a little bit! Now let's have a hug..." That got the cleric two sets of glares. "Um, a handshake?"

Selvi didn't back down, but she didn't push forward either. Folding her arms against her chest, she said, "Okay, until we get out of here, we work together. No longer'n that."

"Agreed." The half-elf sneered.

The school library was a single room, though that word hardly did it justice. It was slightly better to say that it had no walls, only shelf after shelf of books that meandered around the open space like a children's game of dominoes. All it would take was one push, and the whole series would come tumbling down. From the look of things, this may have happened in the past, on more than one occasion.

"You! What mean you here?" the librarian's voice thundered from on high. It was rumored among the student body that Mistress Heyerwif was half-giant by birth, and the woman was in fact taller than anyone else in the school. There was an entire series of shelves set into the ceiling which only she could reach properly. Long blonde hair was pulled back into a bun, and icy blue eyes pinned the gaggle of princesses in place. "Should be home, all of you!"

"Um, our apologies, ma'am," Cassandrella said nervously. "We, we aren't going home this summer. A problem with the Wayhouses..."

"And we've already got extra work to do!" Bianca complained loudly. "Can you believe it? We have to do an in-depth report on the school. Like, twenty or thirty pages each!"

"Ja, ja, that sounds like milady.." Mistress Heyerwif was nodding, and some of the disapproval had vanished from her eyes. "Und so you are needing books, ja? Anyt'ing pertaining to the school?"

"Yes, please," the five princesses said, more or less as a group. Selvi was scowling at the mere mention of more schoolwork.

"Um, we're all taking different topics for it," said Bianca. "History, famous students, geography, local animals, architecture, whatever there is."

"Hm. Let us see what we can find, ja?" The librarian closed her eyes and whispered the words to a spell. Her fingers twisted and turned in complicated patterns, and suddenly tiny blue balls of light danced between them. Mistress Heyerwif

cast the lights into the air, and away they went.
"Follow the guides," she commanded. "They will
find the books you seek."

The princesses babbled their thanks and
rushed off. The tall, blonde woman chuckled as
they went.

"Okay, here we are," Gwenevrael said,
pointing to a spot on the map.

"You sure?" Selvi didn't sound too certain
herself. The old chart was a complicated work of
art, but it looked like it valued that artistry over
accuracy. The section the ranger princess had
pointed out included a fanciful picture of a dragon,
for one thing.

"Pretty sure. Here's that mountain to the
west, the one with two peaks that you can see
from the higher towers. The shape's pretty
distinctive."

"So where does that put us?" asked Flora.
She was leafing through a book of animals common
to the region.

"About a hundred miles north of the nearest big city."

"Pft, that's nothing." Selvi snorted at the thought.

"It's not us that I am worried about." Gwenevrael nodded to the witch and the cleric, who were curled up on the rug, napping. Jinkies was draped under Bianca's chin like a fuzzy neck-warmer.

"Hey! Sleeping beauties! Wake up!" yelled the half-orc. Selvi stomped her feet as hard as she could, rousing such a noise that the two girls and the little cat all jumped straight up in the air.

"That was mean," said Gwenevrael.

"Don't say you weren't thinkin' about it," the barbarian countered. "I can tell you're wantin' to smile."

"Am not!"

"So, um." Bianca yawned. "Where's the fire? Have we figured out where we're going yet?"

"The city of Himmel's Gate. Or maybe Gote. Goat?" Selvi scratched her head. "Am I the only one havin' trouble readin' this thing?"

"It *is* a bit old-fashioned," Gwenevrael

acknowledged. "But it's the best we've got. Going to be a long walk," she warned.

"Oh, that's all right. I've got my broom."

"Thought that was locked up in the teachers' lounge," said Cassandrella, who was still rubbing the moon-dust of sleep from her eyes.

"Yup, which is why you're going to help me get it out!"

"I'm going to do what now?" The cleric shook the last of the fog from her head. "No! That's stealing! As the princess of the Moon I must fight for Truth and Justice, not Petty Larceny!"

"Aww... but it's not stealing," said Bianca. "It's mine, and I'm just, er, liberating it. Then we can use it instead of our feet, so we won't slow everyone else down as much." The witch hooked her arm around Cassandrella's shoulder and made soaring motions with her free hand. "Just think, flying gently through the night, under the light of a big, full moon...."

The cleric's eyes much like the moon at that thought, big and round and shiny. "Oooooooh......"

"So the two of you should go do that," said Gwenevrael. "The rest of us will scout the walls to see where we should sneak out. Meet us by the old oak tree in an hour, okay?"

"In the name of the Moon, we shall be there!"

"Right-o, Gwen. Um, where'd Jinkies go off to?" There was a pitiful mewling from above. Bianca looked up to find her kitty dangling from the parlor's unlit chandelier. "Jinkies! Get down from there this instant!"

"Mrrow?"

"Yes, right now!"

The witch would later claim that the cat's choice of landing spots was completely out of her control, but Selvi still didn't forgive her for a long time after. If anyone had asked the cat — which of course no one had — they would have learned that the little feline liked the smell of the half-orc's hair. That's why he'd aimed directly for her braided scalp with all four sets of claws leading the way.

The woods behind the main keep of the Academy were surprisingly large for something found within castle walls. Gwenevrael had often wondered why Lady Amberyll even bothered. The mess of trees and brush would only help invaders if the castle were attacked. Then again, if the maps were right then there was nobody around to attack the school, and as Bianca had discovered firsthand, there were magical defenses in place as well.

"Wishin' we could just go through the front gate," Selvi groused. "Prolly be safer."

"When was the last time you saw that way to be open?" the ranger replied. "Everything always comes through the Wayhouse doors. In any case, the heaviest defenses would need to be there as well. Watching spells, guardians, stuff like that. If we sneak over the wall back here, we're less likely to trip something."

"Mebbe, mebbe not," said the half-orc. "Don't forget what happened to the witchy-girl."

"Trust me, I haven't. She was flying high over the walls. We won't be."

"So what are we looking for?" asked Flora.

Gwenevrael thought about it. "A spot where the trees block the view of the wall, when seen from the keep, and where there's a safe place to climb to on the other side."

Flora nodded, then cupped her hands. As

she held them up near her face, Mr. Chitters hopped on. The druid let out a long string of clicks and squeaks, sometimes puffing up her cheeks to help get the sounds right.

"Um, she's talkin' to the squirrel again..."

"Shush; let her do her thing."

Mr. Chitters was listening intently, with every sign of understanding more of the conversation than either princess. He gave a high-pitched "Chook!" and leapt from his mistress's hands, bounding off into the woods.

"Follow that squirrel!" shouted Flora. She took off after her pet, leaving the other two princesses to stare at her trail of dust.

"Look, it'll be easy," said Bianca. "Most of the teachers are off to one place or another, just like the other princesses. The rest are more like Mistress Heyerwif and never leave their part of the Academy 'cept for emergencies. We just need to do this fast."

The two girls were hiding around the corner

from the entrance to the main teachers' lounge, which was tucked into one corner of the third floor. There was no sign that anyone was inside.

"Alright. Jinkies?" The little black cat perked at the sound of her voice. "Go reconnoiter."

"Mrow?"

Bianca sighed. "Go check it out."

"Mrewl!"

"Pretty please? With anchovies on top?"

The cat considered for a moment, then padded away nonchalantly, as if it were by mere coincidence that he was going the way she had asked. He nosed around the door, sniffing and rubbing his chin against the hard wood. With a yawn, he sat down in a pool of sunlight that poured in from a nearby window, rolled over on his back, and stretched.

"Um... so, is it okay?" asked Cassandrella.

"It'd better be, or someone's not getting his treat tonight." Bianca tiptoed up to the door and tried the handle. "Locked," she said.

"Should we go get someone with a key?"

"You're not quite getting the idea here,

Cassie. Only a teacher would have the key, but if it's locked, then at least no one's probably in there." Bianca sighed. "Didn't want to have to do this, but..."

The witch searched her pockets, coming up with a pin and a thin scrap of paper. Her usual smile had turned upside down.

"What are you..."

"Shhh. This is a spell that Gran'Mama taught me, so be quiet before I chicken out." She heard Cassie squeak in surprise right as she stabbed her thumb with the pin. A single drop of blood was squeezed out onto the paper. Bianca pressed the scrap to the door, where it stuck as if glued.

"By the pricking of my thumbs, something sneaky this way comes," the witch intoned. "Open locks, whoever knocks!" Lightly, she tapped on the door three times, and heard the bolts turn inside it. With a click, it opened.

She motioned to Cassie, who was staring at her. "Well, shall we?"

"W... w... that was witchcraft!"

"So it was. I'm a witch. What of it? Really, the broom and the hat should've been a tip-off."

"B-but, I thought that was all for show! To be cool or something. Ev-everyone knows witches are..."

"Can we continue this some other time, when we're not standing in front of doors we shouldn't be going through?" Bianca grabbed the cleric and dragged her into the lounge.

The room was shabbier than she'd expected, full of threadbare old couches and stuffed chairs. There were cabinets for holding letters or papers, and a flat mirror on one table that she recognized as having a facsimile charm on it.

"Hold on a moment." She crept over to where the files were stored.

"What are you doing?" Cassie hissed at her.

Bianca ignored the cleric. Flipping through the alphabet of labels, she came across her own name and pulled the file. She took a clean sheet of paper and placed it under the mirror, then pressed the main page of her file against the glass. She'd seen something like this before, and the memory rattled through her head like a many-sided die rolling a high number. There was a light buzz of magic at work, and the mirror flashed with a light that wasn't there. When she retrieved the paper from under it, the blank page was filled with

Mistress Penskill's crabbed handwriting. Quickly, she copied the second page as well.

"Always wanted to know what the old bat thought of me," she said.

"Can we get out of here soon," pleaded Cassie. The poor thing's knees were trembling.

"Okay, okay, hold your bunnies." Bianca slipped over to the closet door. At this distance, she could feel the presence of her beloved broom within. She pulled at the latch, but it wouldn't open.

"Are you going to stick yourself again?"

"I can only do that trick once a day," she answered. "Watch the door, okay?"

The lock on this door wasn't nearly as good as the one on the main door. Focusing her magic onto her singular lock of white hair, she made it grow and stretch, then directed it to slip around the edges of the door. It took a bit of fumbling, and she could feel her control slipping by the end, but she managed to jimmy the door open.

And there it was. Her broom. A yard and a half of polished elm wood with a leather saddle running half its length, fitted to allow for two riders if they didn't mind being close. "Yes!" she cried softly, hugging it.

"Okay, time to go," she said to the cleric. "And I owe you a moonlit ride for coming with me here."

"Yeah..." Cassie didn't sound too happy about that anymore. Also: "Were you crying?"

"No!"

"Only, there's a tear on your cheek."

"It's dusty in here, that's all..."

Jinkies blinked as his mistress and her silly friend shut the door and quietly slipped down the hall. Flicking his ears, which was to him what a shrug was to a human, he got up from his comfortable spot in the sun and followed them.

"Okay, so whaddawe got?" Selvi asked of the assembled princesses. Since they'd already gone through the trouble of making their bags already, it hadn't taken long to put together some basic travel packs. Only Cassandrella had really complained about leaving most of the clothing behind.

Five packs were gathered under the old oak tree, though one was technically hanging from a floating broomstick. Selvi's own bag was sensibly done, as was the half-elf's, though she hated to give Princess Pointy-Ears any sort of compliment. The others... were serviceable, if hard to understand. Selvi'd never seen anything like some of the things sticking out of them.

"Got my broom, my cauldron, and my magic rod," announced Bianca. "I'm good to go!"

"What does the rod do?" Cassandrella asked, eyeing it nervously.

"Darned if I know, but I'm going to figure it out eventually."

"How 'bout you, Moonie?" asked Selvi.

"My travel robes, my moon-silver chain vest, and my moon scepter. For Love and Justice!" The girl twirled the scepter in the air.

"... Right. And you, Flora?"

The druid's pack was almost as pragmatic as hers, except for the lute and the staff planted in the ground next to it. That last one was the real oddity. Selvi could about swear that the thing was growing branches.

"My Staff of Plenty," said Flora. "Once it's

set in the earth, it cannot be moved by anything or anyone except another druid. If given time, it will form branches and give us delicious fruit for breakfast."

"Handy," commented Gwenevrael. "And between myself and Selvi, we've got enough rope, canvas, and other materials to make camping a snap."

"I got a big picnic basket from the kitchen!" Cassandrella announced. "Mistress Fresnelding felt sorry for us getting stuck here."

"Good. Let's get goin' then," said the barbarian. "Times a-wastin'."

According to the druid's tree-rodent, the best spot to slip over the wall was along the southeast edge of the school grounds. Frankly, she wasn't so sure. There were some decent handholds, including a large dent in the stones about twenty feet up, but it wouldn't be an easy climb for at least two of them — and that wasn't even counting the need to get the packs over.

"Well, girls. This is going to take a plan. Any ideas?"

After a fair amount of discussion, a fair bit more of arguing, and some fairly crude sketches in the dirt, they had one.

"What." Uncle's face in this moment was a perfect picture. His eyebrows had levitated all the way up to the hairline, and his jaw had dropped just as far in the opposite direction. Under his right eye, the muscles along the cheekbone had bunched up and were twitching slightly. All of this had come from a single look at the plan, laid out carefully on a piece of scratch paper in colored pencil. The game had adjourned for a few minutes while he'd gone to the toilet and refilled his root beer, but then he'd returned to find... this. "Are you serious?"

"It's a good plan!" Helen insisted.

"Definitely gonna work," said Cynthia.

"And didn't you tell us we should pool our resources?" added Shelby.

"Yes, but..." But he hadn't imagine anything like the Rube Goldberg scenario before him now. Okay, maybe it wasn't quite so bad as that, but it was close. "So... Bianca's going to fly up the wall, but not over it..."

"That's right!"

"And she's going to use her mud ball spell to fill a space in the rocks—" One that he'd intended to be used for a grapnel... "—and then stick Flora's Staff of Plenty in *sideways*?"

Katelyn nodded.

"You said that nothing could move it once it was planted," Shelby pointed out. "And it's magic, so 'nothing' could include gravity, right?"

"Before that," he continued, rubbing his head, "You'll wrap a section of canvas around the staff, rolled up at the edges, and once it's stuck in the wall you'll hang a rope over it and use it as a pulley to lift all your gear up the wall?"

"Once Gwen and Flora have used it to climb up," said Helen.

"Cassie and Bianca are using the broom to get to the top, but not go over," said Claire. "So we don't set off the gargoyles. Probably."

"Then Selvi uses her awesome barbarian strength to hoist up the supplies, so everyone can unload them on top. She'll follow on up, and then we'll lower a rope down the other side to climb down," Shelby said. "Piece of cake."

"If you say so..." Honestly, he could think of a lot of ways this could go wrong, not to mention several things he could do as the game master to actively prevent them from succeeding. Things he probably should do, like point out that the mud ball spell shouldn't produce enough mud to make this work, just to keep things within the letter of the rules. But... it was the most creative thing he'd seen from them so far, and it wasn't even the craziest thing he'd ever seen in a game. Plus, he could smell the pizzas cooking in Max's oven.

His stomach made the decision for him. "Okay, I'll allow it. Time to roll 'em, ladies. Katelyn, Bianca's skill bonus for flying is going to be canceled out by having to balance Cassie on there as well, so you will need to secure her somehow. Cynthia, Flora doesn't have any points in climbing, so use her strength bonus when you roll. There's no rush on most of this, so if at first you don't succeed, I'll let you take ten. That is," he explained, "we'll imagine it takes longer than normal, but you do finally reach the top. Okay, let's roll."

The view from the wall was actually rather nice, Gwenevrael thought. The forest extended a long ways into the distance, where it met the hazy purple outline of the eastern mountains. Her eyes picked out more landmarks, matching them to the map in her hands. There was the lake, and the river... She relaxed. Everything seemed accurate so far.

Behind her, she could hear Selvi grunting as she pulled Flora up the last few feet. The druid had gone back down to retrieve her staff, but then needed help getting back while holding on to the cumbersome thing.

"So, we ready to go?" asked Bianca. The witch had somehow managed to ferry Cassandrella without dropping her, though the cleric had not liked the idea of being strapped in by magically animated hair. The moon princess's face was green like cheese as Bianca's white lock released her, and she fell off the broom and onto the stone of the walls.

"Just a moment..." Cassandrella burped. "Not feeling so good..."

The ranger secured the rope onto a stone fixture, after first making sure it wasn't a gargoyle or otherwise some potential defense of the school, and tossed it off the other side. The rope didn't quite reach the bottom, but it came within a few feet. Nearby, Flora's squirrel chittered at her.

"Okay; you were right, sir squirrel. I am sorry to have doubted you," she said in a low voice.

The last thing she needed was for Selvi to see her talking with the little red rodent.

Getting back down the wall on the other side wasn't nearly as difficult, though once again they had to secure Cassandrella properly before lowering her down in the same manner as the packs. The moon princess was not happy by the time they got her to the ground, but at least they were all outside the walls now.

She nodded to Selvi, and the half-orc nodded back. The two of them hefted their packs and helped the magic-users with theirs. Then, as a group, they began their adventure.

"And it's time for a pizza break!" Uncle announced. "Katelyn, that was some very good role-playing with Bianca, and Claire? You added some excellent details in. We're going to have to capitalize on those in the future."

"My princess didn't get to do much," said Cynthia with a pout.

"We'll just have to fix that after we have our pizza, eh?" Uncle winked. "Don't worry; you're headed into a forest. Druids always have things to do in the forest. And," he added before Shelby could form the words. "There will be fights. It's time for some action."

"Good." The black-haired girl nodded at that.

"Enjoying it so far?"

"Yeah, Uncle!" "Uh-huh!" "... yes." "Super-fantastic!" "It's okay."

"Thanks for the ringing endorsement, ladies."

Max had the pies set on the neighboring table, and the ravenous horde of princess players migrated in that direction with nary a complaint. Uncle tidied the game table, swapping out a generic forest map for the one of the castle, and made some notes from the safety of his game-master's screen. The sturdy cardboard divider was what hid most of the game's important information from the players, and in his head Uncle imagined a scene that must have played out behind closed doors, where no princesses were allowed.

"And there they go." Mistress Penskill tapped the edge of her magic mirror, making the image within both larger and clearer. The Academy's main instructor in the arts arcane was short and round, with bright aqua hair and a serious, sour face that did not jive with her gnomish heritage at all. She shook her head as she watched the five young students disappear into the forest. "Is this really such good idea, to let them off the leash like this?"

"It will be pleasingly quiet here, ja?" said Mistress Heyerwif. "Those girls would find some trouble und make us all go crazy."

"They will need to learn how to work together, to trust one another," said Lady Amberyll. The headmistress leaned back in her chair and massaged her temples. "That is not something we can teach at this institution. If we were to try, we would most likely achieve the opposite result. No, no," she said. "Let it be their own choices which instruct them. We shall enjoy the show, and intervene only if absolutely necessary."

Mistress Penskill nodded, and the image in the mirror faded away. "Still can't believe that little pipsqueak had the temerity to steal copies from our files."

"I did warn you." Lady Amberyll's eyes glittered with amusement. "That is why we only put what we wanted her to see in that file, was it not?"

"Sure, sure. Hope you know what game you're playing here. That one's grandmother is no joke."

"Neither am I, Penelope. Neither am I."

Pizza Time!

"Okay!" Uncle called. "Are we ready to keep going?"

A low rumble of general assent floated to his ears from the far side of the table, fueled by pizza grease and sugary drinks. Everyone had certainly had their fill of Max's signature pepperoni-plus pizza. He would have to step things up before they went into a food coma.

"So, to recap: Five young princesses, played by you ladies, have just snuck out of school because you all didn't want to be stuck there for the entire summer. As far as the game is concerned, that all happened yesterday now. You managed to make decent time that first day, then Gwen and Selvi set up camp for the night. Next day, you get up fairly early and keep going. So now you're in the middle of a big wild forest. What are you going to do?"

He expected Cynthia to chime in first, or Helen. Their princesses certainly had the most skills related to traveling through the woods. Shelby was also a possibility, since the girl had been taking charge a lot so far. But no, once again his expectations were dashed upon the reality that these kids were nothing like him, and certainly were not playing the game the same way.

"We stop at noon to have a picnic!" Claire shouted before anyone else could say anything.

"A... picnic."

"Yeah! We got a picnic basket from the school kitchen, and it was so full of stuff that we couldn't eat it all yesterday, so today we should have a picnic!"

"Wouldn't we eat it all for breakfast?" said Shelby.

"That's a very good po—"

"But Flora's got that magic staff!" Cynthia interrupted him. "We'd have lots of fresh fruit for breakfast, so we could save the leftovers for lunch."

Everyone was nodding at this, much to Uncle's annoyance. He looked over the notes behind his divider screen, where the details for a fight with some bandits lay. As encounters went, it was pretty straightforward, especially for level three characters, but he'd wanted to ease the girls into this. Now, though? If they wanted picnics, he'd give them...

Hmm... Uncle keyed in a quick internet search, coming up with all the details he needed before the girls could even finish debating how to do the picnic. "Alright, ladies," he announced. "It's picnic time, with everything that goes along with it."

It was a beautiful day in the forest. The sun shone down on them through the trees, and the birds were singing like a choir of angels. For a temple-raised girl like Princess Cassandrella, it was like a fairy tale turned real. She hopped and skipped merrily down the trail, stopping every few minutes to ask Gwenevrael or Flora for the name of some flower that had caught her eye.

The ranger and the druid put up with her exuberance, though Selvi rolled her eyes every time. The barbarian didn't have much use for flowers.

Bianca was the least happy of the lot, because it turned out that she did have to walk after all. The twisty forest trails were hard to navigate by broom, and she was always either dragging her feet in the dirt or hitting her head on branches. The broom followed her around instead, carrying her pack and Jinkies, who was happily perched on the saddle. How she envied the little fuzzbutt.

"Can we stop and rest for a bit?" she whined. "My feet are killing me!"

"Yeah!" chimed in Cassie. "And it's almost time for lunch, too!"

"We took a break an hour ago," growled Selvi. "Can't you—" She was stopped by Gwenevrael's hand on her shoulder.

"A group travels only as fast as its slowest member," the ranger pointed out. "And it *is* a good time of day to have a meal."

"Picnic time!" crowed the moon princess.

"Yeah, yeah." Selvi brushed the hand away. "Coddle the softies, why dontcha. Their poor widdle toes might fall off their feet, otherwise."

"Really?" Cassandrella sat on the nearest rock, pulled off a boot, and wiggled her toes. "Nope, all present and accounted for!"

"It looks like there might be a clearing ahead," Flora announced, ignoring the discussion entirely. "What's left in the basket?"

There was quite a lot left in the big wicker basket they'd received from the Academy cook. Either Mistress Fresnelding had been extra generous, or she'd overestimated how much the five girls could eat. Flora's Staff of Plenty had produced handfuls of fuzzy brown fruits, all green and juicy on the inside, to break their morning fast, so the bread, cheese, and sausage inside the basket could wait till now.

The glen was perhaps twenty feet across, and its ground was covered with soft green grass. A few rocks poked through the turf, and served as excellent shelves for heavy packs. Selvi unfurled a roll of tent canvas upon the ground, and the five of them settled down for an enjoyable lunch. There were enough sandwich fixings for everyone, with a bit of sausage left over for Jinkies.

Flora had her lute out and was happily assaulting everyone's ears with off-key caroling when she wasn't cramming ham and cheese in her face. Jinkies yowled along a few times.

Yes, a good time was had by all, right up to the moment where cat and squirrel sat up stock straight, with ears pricked and noses twitching.

"Um, Helen? Why's your uncle chuckling like that?" asked Shelby.

"I dunno. Er, Uncle? Uncle..."

It was a huge smile, a massive grin plastered across his face. His friends had often told him never to play poker, which was fine by him. This was more his game, and it was time to pull the ace from his sleeve. "Well, ladies. You wanted a picnic, and where there's a picnic, there's also... them."

"Them?" Cynthia gave him the screwy eye, which only made him grin harder.

"Yup. **Them**."

The princesses were looking every which way, trying to figure out where the trouble was coming from. Something was obviously setting the animals on edge, but what? Selvi and Cassandrella hopped to their feet and looked down the trail, while Gwenevrael's eyes scanned the high tree branches. Flora and Bianca were trying to calm their critters, with little success. Mr. Chitters and Jinkies were shaking from nerves.

And when trouble came, it wasn't from the trail, nor from the trees. With a great push, something forced its way up from under the picnic canvas, sending the two remaining princesses and their pets tumbling away. The canvas jumped and shook, flapping away to reveal... **them**.

Three bodies, each the size of a large dog, covered in reddish brown fuzz. Broad, rounded heads with large, glittery eyes, short antenna, and clicking mandibles. Six skinny, hard-shelled legs, the first two of which sported four-clawed hands with opposable thumbs.

More followed from the hole they'd opened beneath the canvas, pushing up and out with an economy of movement and coordination.

"Ants?!"

"What's a picnic without them?" Uncle laughed. "And now I feel like watching old monster movies. Well, ladies? They caught you off guard. Whatcha gonna do?"

Gwenevrael wasn't sure what to make of... them. They were ants, but on the other hand not. Regular ants weren't three and a half feet long. They also didn't immediately grab people's packs and... wait, what?

"What!?" she shouted. "Stop! Stop them! Selvi! Cassandrella!"

There were ten of them out of the hole now, and they'd paired off to grab the princesses' gear. Faster than anyone could react, the ant-things were hustling their loot away.

"Hey!" Selvi recovered from surprise the fastest, jumping in to block the pair of ants with her pack. In her head, she was cussing long and hard that she'd left her sword next to her stuff. The scimitar was in the hands of them, now.

"Shelby, language."

The black-haired girl just blew him a raspberry.

Selvi Khan's-daughter was a champion of *êl-sakhar*, a sport of the high plains played traditionally with the severed heads of one's enemies, though nowadays it was usually a weighted ball of rags instead. Either way, these ant things weren't nearly as heavy, and with a single swift kick she punted the one with her sword into the nearest tree. As she reclaimed the blade, she could see Princess Point-Ears wresting her bow and quiver from another pair of marauders. Moonie wasn't having as much luck freeing her pack, though it was fun watching her whack a bug over the head repeatedly with her holy symbol and yelling things like "Moon's Justice!"

The witch girl shouted a bunch of words, through their meaning was lost on Selvi's ears. The magic broom understood, apparently, and it leapt from the grasp of an ant-thing. Bianca's pack tried to follow along, pulled by the straps, but a quick snip of the mandibles cut it off. The broom flew freely back to its mistress with the little cauldron dangling from it. The rest of the pack disappeared down the trail with the ants.

"After them!" Selvi roared, baring her tusks in anger. How dare these... these bugs steal from them! She would squish their heads beneath her boots, rip their legs from their thoraxes and beat war drum rhythms on their fat, buggy butts! Her rage pushed her forward down the path, paying no attention to the whipping branches or protruding roots, or —

Something slammed into her from behind, forcing her to the ground. She almost sent a fist smashing right into the other person's face before she realized it was Princess Pointy-Ears.

Oh, who was she kidding? Selvi wanted to punch the half-elf anyway.

"What are you..." she began, but Gwenevrael shushed her and pointed up. A rather large and heavy-looking log came swinging across the trail and through the space where Selvi would have been. A second later, it swung back, not quite as fast.

"Those buggies are smarter than they look,"

the ranger said. "Had their escape planned out really well."

"Er, yeah." As her anger and rage receded, Selvi was realizing just how dumb she'd been. This did not make her any happier. "Thanks," she said through gritted teeth.

"Don't get me wrong," said Gwenevrael. "I still don't like you, and I know you still don't like me, but if we're going to get our stuff back then we shall need to work together." The half-elf offered a gloved hand. "A continued truce?"

Selvi took the hand and shook it. "Yeah, for now."

"So what did we lose?" Gwenevrael asked, once everyone was back in the clearing.

"All of our packs," Flora reported, "and the picnic basket, too. They tried to take my Staff of Plenty, but couldn't get it out of the ground. Left the canvas," she added as an afterthought.

"At least we got our weapons," growled Selvi. Gwenevrael could only nod at that.

"Got my broom, too!" Bianca announced. "But... but..." The little witch's eyes began to tear up. "My magic rod was in my pack! Gran'Mama gave it to me and told me to keep it safe and be a smart girl and figure it out and now she's going to be so **mad** and what am I going to do? WAAAAAAAHH!" She broke down as the other princesses stared.

Cassandrella plopped down to the witch's left, and Flora to her right, then the two of them squished her in the middle of the biggest hug they could manage. The sniffly sobs were smothered in folds of homespun cotton and shimmery moon-silk.

"Okay, okay. Mushy stuff aside," said Selvi. "What are we doin' to get our stuff back?" The barbarian growled. "Shoulda kept chasin' them."

"And you'd soon have discovered just how many traps they've set on that trail."

"Yeah, yeah. Rub it in, why dontcha."

"If you would permit this intrusion, ladies..." A voice, long and sinuous on the vowels and slightly lisped on the esses, slipped through the mass of trees behind the princesses to surprise them as a light tickle on the ears.

Selvi had her scimitar up and ready, and Gwenevrael had an arrow nocked before the last ess could finish.

There was something standing in the shadows of the trees, though not even the half-elf's keen eyes could pick out the details at first. Some magic had kept it hidden from their sight, and that same magic made this person blurry and shadowed even as it walked towards them. Once the figure reached the sunlight of the clearing, the magic was dispelled, and the five princesses got a good look at their visitor.

The... person stood tall like a man, almost as tall as Princess Selvi, but was like nothing they'd ever seen before. The body was stocky, with short legs and long arms, and its fingers and toes alike were tipped with thick claws. Its face was snout-like, with long lips and a tiny nose. A scaly plate of natural armor spread from its forehead, over its crown, and down its back. Tufts of fur stuck out between the scales. A broad tail hung behind it, also scaled. This newcomer looked nothing so much like a pangolin crossed with a human.

"A what-o-lin?" asked Shelby.

"Yeah, what's that?" chimed in Claire. Behind her huge glasses, the girl's eyes twinkled curiously.

"Sounds familiar..." said Cynthia.

"Yanno, a pangolin," said Uncle. "They've got some down at the zoo. Kind of like an armadillo, but with scales instead of banded armor. They can roll up into balls," he added.

"Aw yeah, that's the one!"

-tickety tappety tap- Uncle had his laptop out. "Look, this is what I'm talking about," he said, pulling up a Wikipedia page for the animals. That was followed by an internet video of baby pangolins for the girls to coo over while he grabbed some more root beer.

"Okay, ladies," he said when he returned. "Whatcha gonna do?"

"Attack it!" said Shelby.

"No!" said Helen. "He hasn't done anything yet."

"He was pretty polite..." added Claire.

"... let's ask."

"Okay!" said Shelby. "My princess doesn't lower her sim, shim..."

"Scimitar."

"Right. Doesn't lower her simmy-tar, but she asks him what he's doing. Um, it is a 'him', right?"

Uncle shrugged. "Hard to say, just by looking. The voice sounds more masculine, though. Anyhoo, the pangolin-man greets you again, and introduces himself as L'shoop-floopshup."

"Wow, say that again!" Claire said.

"L'shoopfloopshup."

"Ten times fast!" demanded Helen.

"L'shoopfloopshuplshoopshupfloopshup..."
Uncle screwed his face up, crossed his eyes, and
stuck out his tongue, much to the amusement of
the girls.   "But you can call him Louis," he said.
"Please."

"Okay, um, Louis," said Gwenevrael as she
relaxed the hold on her bowstring. The magically
produced arrow shaft flickered and disappeared,
no longer necessary. "It is good to hear a friendly
voice, but I must ask. What are you doing here?"

"If I may?" The pangolin man sat on the dirt
with his tail curled up around his legs. "I am
traveling with a band of my brothers and sisters.
We wander the world, hunting down tasty insects
for food and sport. Perhaps you can guess where
this is heading?"

"Them," Flora said with a scowl. "The ants.
They ain't natural, are they?   Something felt
wrong."

"Ah yes, you are a daughter of the woods,
are you not? No, the ant-men, as they be, are not
a result of nature's path, though if I am to be
honest, neither are my people."

"The forest ain't afraid of you, though."

Beside the druid, Mr. Chitters gave his squeak of approval.

"And happy am I to hear that. The truth is, my comrades and I have been tracking this contingent of the ant-men for some time now. They appear to have settled in these woods, and we believe they are preparing to contact their queen at the home hive. Should that happen, then an invasion may be imminent. It occurs to me that, as natives of this land and recent victims of their rapacious nature, you might desire some aid and give the same in return?"

"What the heck's that supposed to mean?" asked Selvi.

"He's saying that we can all help each other," said the ranger.

"Why doesn't he just do it himself?" The half-orc eyed the pangolin man suspiciously.

"It is enough to say that the numbers do not favor my band," said Louis. "The workers are of little concern, were there not so many of them. Then there are the warriors, which are a much more difficult matter. And the leader of the outpost, well... Even with the assistance of you ladies, we will have our hands busy."

"But we'll get our stuff back?" asked Bianca. The tears had dried, but her eyes were still red and angry.

"That, and whatever else you may want

from their hoard," promised Louis. "My people's objective is death to the ants. We care not for the rest."

Gwenevrael nodded. "I think we can agree to these terms." Beside her, Selvi wasn't looking happy, but the barbarian wasn't saying no, either.

"Good." Louis hopped to his feet and bowed. "If you would follow me to my camp, where we can rest and prepare?"

The princesses grabbed everything that was left to them and followed the pangolin man into the forest.

"So when you get to his camp," Uncle was saying, "you see six more of Louis's friends doing various things. They don't all look like him; some are more armadillo-ish, while others look like anteaters, or even hedgehogs. They introduce themselves, but all the names are just as hard to pronounce."

"What are we doing now?" asked Cynthia.

"Preparing, I guess," Claire answered.

"But how?"

Shelby raised her hand. "I'm gonna talk with someone to make battle plans."

"Magic users should also take time to make sure their spells are ready," Uncle noted. "Er, yes?" Katelyn was tugging on his sleeve. "What is it?" The girl pointed to a note on her sheet. "Okay, Bianca can make some potions, too. One of Louis's friends will help there."

"I'll ask Mr. Chitters to help me find some animals to help us!" offered Cynthia.

"Gwen will go with Selvi to talk with Louis and his boss," said Helen.

Uncle clapped his hands. "Well then, sounds like we've got stuff to do!"

"Fifty buggers, you say?" Selvi was staring at a rough map of the area, drawn in reddish-brown ink on animal skin. It was simply done, with little triangles for trees and circles for rocks, but it still looked more accurate than the one the princesses had.

"Plus five warriors, the leader, and three others besides." Louis's leader was a long-nosed, shaggy person, with light cream and brown fur. His voice was booming and nasal, and his name had been officially shortened to Phil.

"What others?" Gwenevrael leaned in, tracing the map with one of her knives.

"The leader caste of the ant-men like to keep pets," explained Louis. "A few days back, they caught a few bandits. The fools were trying to steal food, I imagine. In any case, they're working for the bugs now, whether they like it or not."

"Which is why your assistance is appreciated," said Phil. "The three pets are strong in ways we cannot work well against. But they do not see well in the dark, which is why we shall wait till late in the evening to attack."

The ranger nodded. "I can see in the darkness, and I believe half-orcs can as well, right?"

Selvi grunted.

"That still leaves the others, though..."

Claire had her hand raised and waving frantically. The tips of her oversized hair ribbon wobbled like a pair of floppy ears.

"Yes, Claire?" Uncle didn't quite sigh.

"Since my magic is all holy moon power and stuff, do I have a spell that lets people see in the dark?"

"No, that's not actually a cleric's spell usually..."

"Can I ask for it anyway?" She pulled

nervously on her glasses.

"Ask me?"

"No, ask the Moon." The little girl stood on her seat so they could look eye to eye. "Can I ask the Moon for a spell like that?"

Uncle considered for a moment, then made a quick calculation on a piece of scrap paper. "Okay. Since your goddess is actually in the sky right now, visible and about half full, I guess you can ask her for a boon. Roll your big one, add in your wisdom modifier — that's a plus three, by the way — and we shall see."

A goldenrod orange twenty-sided die clattered across the table, coming up 19.

"Whew..." Uncle whistled. "And with the modifier, that's a twenty-two. Okay then, you get a new trick in your level two spell slot, instead of one use of Align Weapon. It's called, um..."

"Moon Eyes Shine Bright!"

"Er, sure. Let's go with that. It grants low-light vision to yourself and two other people, for one night."

"Thanks, Uncle game-dude!"

Uncle stacked his papers together and knocked them against the table to get them in order. "Okay then, shall we begin?"

Flora sat on a tree stump at the edge of the camp, listening to the sound of the woods. Birdsong had faded with the light of day, to be replaced with the buzz of insects. It was easy to meditate and open her mind to the voice of nature — and wow, was it an angry one. She could hear it in the bristling of the pine needles, in shrieks of the hawk and the whining of mosquitoes. There was something in these woods that the woods did not want, and this princess knew what that thing was. She cradled her lute and strummed along to the magic in her head, calling out to all the little ears that were willing to hear.

She'd been right, earlier. Nature absolutely hated those ant-men, as much as it could hate anything. With a pluck and a twang of the lute string, she was telling Nature exactly what was upsetting it, and how to make it stop.

Bianca spent most of the afternoon with a hard-shelled member of the anti-bug squad named Mmshuthrashl. The witch called her Mim. Mim was the healer of the group, and had dozens of little bags of spell components on hand. Bianca's little cauldron was put to good use, and soon she was filling a dozen tiny vials with a light green liquid.

"This one's full of jumping magic," she was explaining to a wide-eyed Cassie. "Slurp one down and you'll be bouncing like a bunny rabbit for a few minutes." She waved to the other colors they'd already finished. "Blue is Mim's special health potion. Everyone's getting two of those."

Cassie took her share of the green and blue, tucking them into the pockets of her moon-silk robe. "What about this?" she asked, reaching for a vial of red liquid.

A pale, slender hand grabbed the cleric's wrist. The little witch was stronger than she looked, and her face was deadly serious. "Mim made that one for me, special. That one's dangerous, and it's all mine," was all she said.

The moon princess looked into her friend's eyes and saw all the tales of witches reflected within them. She couldn't help but shiver a little.

Now it was late into the night. The Moon had come and almost left, sinking slowly behind the mountains. Some of its glow remained in the night sky, along with thousands of twinkling stars. Bianca knew the constellations well, and thanks to Cassie's new spell she could see well enough by their light to navigate above the tree-tops with ease.

To the north, beneath the constellation of the Dragon with its burning red eye, there was a clearing. Flora had described it quite well. All the trees there had recently been chopped down and chewed up by the ant-men, and now a gaping hole opened in the middle.

She was flying over the hole right now. It was a deep black circle in the middle of the dirt and grass. Bianca carefully pulled out her new red potion, held it out at arm's length, and let it fall.

With a *whoomph*, the hole was no longer dark and black. She liked it better in bright red, actually, though she barely dodged the rising fireball.

There was the signal! The fading moonlight was as bright as day thanks to Cassandrella's magic, and to Princess Flora's eyes the explosion was brighter still. She could see ants from where she was perched, high in a tree. Louis said the buggers couldn't see too well by night, and she trusted him on that. She trusted her new furry friends more.

Flora raked her fingers across her lute with a loud twang. As loudly as she could, she sang:

My eyes have seen the horror
Of the coming of the squirrels!
With their sharp-sharp teeth and bushy tails
they aid us pretty girls.
With the rabbits and the deer
they make those buggies hurl!
Fuzzy-wuzzies rule the world!

Not half bad for an afternoon's composition, if she did say so herself. From the bushes all around the clearing, the fuzzy-wuzzies burst into action, descending on the worker ants as they poured from the fiery depths of their hill. Anyone who thought rabbits were weak had never seen a mother bunny take on a snake in defense of her young. Those teeth weren't just there for nibbling carrots!

"Um, thank you for the musical selection, Cynthia," said Uncle. "With your encouragement, all the local squirrels and rabbits are busy biting legs off of workers, while the deer are trampling the bodies." He rolled a die behind his divider screen. "Your 'Battle Hymn of the Fuzzy-Wuzzies' even attracted a badger, which is currently trashing a squad of worker ants by the north end of the clearing." A red piece of plastic marked the spot. "Let's just give him some space, 'kay? Badgers aren't the friendliest sorts."

"Wow, that was awesome!" shouted Cynthia. "Thanks for lettin' me try it."

"No prob, kiddo." Honestly, he'd stretched the definitions of most of the animal-handling spells and skills on that one, but she'd rolled well, and it really was funnier this way. "So, who's up next?"

Arrows flashed overhead, streaking through the air from where Princess Pointy-Ears was hiding. Selvi scowled. Just like an elf to stay in the trees where it was safe. She preferred to get down and dirty. Brandishing her scimitar, Selvi Khan's-daughter screamed defiantly and rushed into the chaos.

Ahead of her, an armadillo man was barreling through the worker ants, leaving wide gaps in the enemy's defenses for her to pass. Behind her, Moonie and the rest of the bug-eaters followed. Her ears told her that, though she kept her eyes forward.

The little bugs were no challenge at all, and dangerous only because they wouldn't stop for anything. Her scimitar cut them down left and right, while her boots stomped bug bits with loud crunches.

One. *Stomp.* Two. *Stomp.* Three. *Stomp...*
This was maybe the most boring fight of her young
life!

With a shriek, more ants swarmed from the
hill. These newcomers were twice the size of the
workers and looked even bigger when they stood
tall and upright on four legs. Thick forearms
wielded nasty-looking spears, shields, or axes.

"Awright!" the barbarian shouted. "Now
that's more like it!"

Unlike the half-orc, Princess Cassandrella
hadn't been in a real fight even once in her entire
life. She had her moon-silver armor, yes, and her
scepter doubled wonderfully as a head-thumper,
but that didn't mean she was in any way prepared.
Mistress Mehl's basic combat course at the
Academy hadn't included anything about giant
bugs, for crying out loud! Someone should make a
complaint, she decided.

But first, there was the problem at hand.
When the warrior ants made their appearance, all
clicking jaws and waving spears, of course she was
scared! Who wouldn't be? And when she was
scared, there was only one thing for a young moon
princess to do. She prayed.

"O Bounteous Moon! Grant me thy light, so I may squish some buggy butt!"

Her blessed mother may not have approved of that prayer, but the Moon didn't seem to mind. Cassandrella's scepter glowed with a soft silver light, and then it was gone, replaced by a piece of the shining moon in the shape of a sword.

"Moonlight Crescent Cut!"

Princess Fiona finished her song with a flourish, to signal that it was time for all fuzzy animals to make themselves scarce. Most of them listened, if they hadn't already scampered away, but that old badger on the north side continued fighting and biting like a hungry man battling for the last plate of flapjacks.

"Stay here, Mr. Chitters," she commanded. "No, you're not coming along," she added when the squirrel chittered back. "You'd just be... What do you mean, I'd be in the way too!?"

She dropped to the ground and hefted her lute. The ants may have made off with her pack and the simple sword within it, but she still had this. It was made of enchanted ironwood, and strong enough to take a hit, or give one. Her favorite uncle had given it to her, along with some magic words. She'd never tried them, but now seemed like as good a time as any...

"*El Kabong!*"

The wood of the lute swelled and stretched, until it was a huge, spiked club. It still weighed the same in her hands, but she bet it would hurt ants just as good as anything else.

"El Kabong?" Shelby had one eyebrow raised in perfect derision. "Seriously?"

"That's the problem with kids these days," groused Uncle. "No appreciation for the classics."

"If you can call it that." The curly-haired girl rolled her eyes. "And what's with all the magic stuff, all of a sudden?"

"Well, I gave you all this cool stuff at the beginning, and not all of it has seen use. Speaking of which, aren't you the least bit curious what **your** special item does?"

All five of the warriors were out and about now, and everyone had their hands full. Louis and Phil had taken on the first, slashing at it with their claws, while the rolling armadillo and a spiky echidna-man fended off another.

Selvi's attention was on the reddish brown monstrosity before her. This warrior bore a sword and shield, both fashioned from some sort of shell. Whatever the stuff was, her blade couldn't get a bite into it. Each hit slid off with a soft clang. She hacked and slashed, only to be parried and blocked at each turn.

It was playing with her! Selvi's moonlit vision began to turn red in fury. How dare it treat her like... like... a child! A weakling! Could it not tell she was a khan's daughter, a warrior by blood!? Rage burned within her, kindling a flame in her chest, centered on the dragonbone talisman around her neck.

The polished knucklebone was carved with the names of her ancestors, great warriors all, and though she couldn't look down to check she was certain that those names now glowed like dragon's fire. The spirits of her forefathers fought with her, she knew, and Selvi pressed on even harder.

And then, to her left and to her right, glowing red forms appeared, bearing arms and armor much like hers. On the left was an orcish warrior, glorious and strong, while on the right was a human of the high plains, with a spiked turban and oiled beard. Both wielded the wickedly curved blades of her homeland, and as one they moved with her.

Try as it might, the warrior ant could not

stop three blades at once. With a wild howl, the barbarian princess pressed the advantage.

"And that's how the ancestral totem power works for you," Uncle was explaining. "The spirits move with you, attack with you, basically give you three sword strokes for the price of one. However, they can't attack things independently, can't leave your side, and they only appear if you're raging while wearing that talisman."

"Okay, whatever." Shelby was trying to keep a cool look on her face, and was failing. "I'm gonna keep attacking on my next turn."

"Alright. But first, could you roll your big one for me?" Uncle asked. "Everyone else, too?"

Shelby gave him her best puzzled-but-who-cares-what-you-think look, but rolled anyway. The red twenty-sider rattled across the table, coming up 8. Everyone else rolled much higher, except for Claire's piddling 2.

"This was a perception check. It's meant to see if you're paying attention to other stuff in battle. The leader and her pets have just arrived." He placed a chess king, two knights, and a bishop on the table, not far from Selvi's pawn. "Unfortunately, a certain barbarian princess is too busy hacking things up to notice."

Selvi Khan's-daughter felt on top of the world. With furious howls she was slowly wearing down the warrior ant, and she anticipated with glee the final strike that would sent its buggy carcass to the ground in pieces.

Then the wind picked up. It blew in hard from her right, raising trails of dust and leaves. A second later, she was off her feet, blown head over heels by a blast of rushing air. Her rage was broken by the distraction, and the two phantom fighters disappeared with it.

Up above, Princess Bianca saw everything. She saw where a new hole opened in the earth, and she saw the three human forms climb out to herald the arrival of the ant leader. She saw one of the former bandits raise a rod — **her** rod! — and blast Selvi with a huge gust of wind.

Most importantly, she saw how he did it.

Her magic lock of white hair grew long, draping down to the ground. With great care, she eased her broom forward, letting the hair float quietly along until it was brushing against the rod in the bandit's hand. Then, like a snake, she struck. Her hair plucked the magic heirloom from the man's surprised grasp.

The leader ant noticed her, raising its buggy head in all its horribly buggy glory. Compared to the warriors, it was slender, almost dainty, with a tapered body and smaller mandibles. Its antennae were long and swept-back, and a series of horny bumps circled the flat space of its head like a tiara. With her improved vision, she could see the strangely human hands on the end of those ant arms make arcane gestures. Sparks of light began to circle its wrists.

Oh, no. Bianca wasn't about to let a buggy wizard get the drop on her. She aimed her rod at it, tracing her fingers across the golden inlay the way she'd seen the bandit mage do, and —

Her world seemed to shatter as strange patterns filled her brain. Everything was precise and geometric, formed of pure shapes linked by the lightning of consciousness. It was too alien, too much, too loud inside her skull.

Bianca fell from her broom like a stone.

Gwenevrael had stopped shooting arrows

when Louis and their allies had moved in. Even with her elven eyesight, she couldn't be sure about her targets in all this chaos. It was all good, though; she still had her sword.

As did Cassandrella, the ranger was surprised to see. The moon princess was holding her own against a swarm of workers, waving around a blade of silvery light as if she actually knew how to use it. The weapon did not seem to cut the ants, but by their reactions it was obvious something was hurting them.

Then a taller shadow loomed over the cleric. One of the warrior ants had come to the aid of its lesser brethren, and Cassandrella did not seem to notice the monster's axe as it was raised in her direction.

Gwenevrael would have cursed if she'd had the time to spare. Instead, she quickly drank one of Bianca's potions, a green one that almost made her gag. The stuff tasted like pure, concentrated awful, but it worked. She could feel the power in her legs as she leapt and bounded across the field, hurdling over worker ants and occasionally using them as springboards. The ranger landed next to the cleric just in time to deflect the warrior's axe with her own sword.

"I've got your back," she told the surprised princess. "Let's waste this one together."

Cassandrella nodded, and together they rushed the warrior. She jumped high, bringing her sword down on the ant's shield with a clash, while the moon princess took the opening and stabbed it in the thorax with her weapon. "Lovely Lunar Fixation!" the cleric cried as the oversized ant screamed in pain.

Gwenevrael was caught in the chest by a flailing arm — the one with the shield, thankfully. The blow knocked the wind out of her, but she still managed to duck and roll, coming back on her feet almost immediately. The ant was hacking at Cassandrella, but the cleric was hopping like a crazed bunny rabbit, just barely dodging the first blow, then the second, only to get hit in the face by the shield.

With the last lingering effect of the potion's jumpiness empowering in her legs, Gwenevrael drew her daggers and leapt for the warrior's back. The bug wore a metal collar to protect its thin neck, but that wasn't much good for it now. The ranger brought her two daggers across the collar, and the neck snapped.

The rest of the ant collapsed to the ground with a thud.

"Are you alright?" Flora asked as she pulled Selvi up. Her lute had returned to its original form for now, though it proved more than good enough to bat a worker ant away all by itself.

Selvi wasn't sure how to answer. The heat of her rage had faded away, and now she felt cold inside. If the druid weren't right there to see it, she could have puked her guts out. "Er, yeah. Just fine and dandy," she lied. "Where's everyone else?"

"Cassie and Gwen are holding off one of the warrior ants, that way." Flora pointed to the south. "Louis's people took out most of the rest, so now they're working on the leader."

"Wha.. Where's the one I was fighting?" If someone else had stolen her glory, oh...

"It retreated to the other side of the hill, I think. Somewhere that way, at least. Looked like it was hurting plenty from the way you mauled it."

"Hmph." There was some satisfaction in that, at least. "What about witchy-girl?"

The druid shrugged. "Not sure. Saw her fall off her broom a little while back. Found you first, though."

"Might as well look for her, then." Selvi winced as her armor moved across several new bruises. "Gotta stick together'n all that." Her ears pricked at the sound of muted cursewords. "Okay, think she's over that way."

Selvi led the way, batting buggies right and left with Flora bringing up the rear.

Bianca was having the worst headache of her life. What had happened? Had the ant leader got her with some sort of magic attack? All she knew was that she would do anything for some of Gran'Mama's special headache cure right now, even though she knew exactly what the old bat put in it.

Up above, she could hear Jinkies mewling from the back of the broom. Without her, the flying stick was circling in a holding pattern, awaiting her command. It could wait a little longer, she decided. At least until she could stand up straight without seeing double.

There were four people running up to her. No, wait. Two people. Selvi and Flora, in fact. Weakly, she waved.

"Hey, ladies. Got my magic rod back." Her voice sounded addled, even to her own ears. "Gran'Mama will be so happy with me."

"Good going... oh, crap!" shouted Selvi. The barbarian raised her scimitar.

Down the slope a ways, three figures could be seen stumbling through the evening dark. The leader ant's pets were having a difficult time of it, as the grass was now covered in bits of ant, and their eyes weren't as keen or as enchanted as the princesses'. They should have been cussing away every time they stepped in a puddle of buggy guts, but instead the three bandits were strangely quiet.

"I got 'em," Bianca declared, aiming her rod at the first bandit. It only shook a little in her hands as she brought its magic to life. "Take this!" she shouted.

The bandit stopped dead in his tracks and screamed. Dropping his sword, he doubled over and clutched at the ground as his silhouette expanded and grew in the dim light of the evening. When he stood again, he was over twelve feet tall, and all of his gear had similarly grown with him.

"Um, so your grandmother gave you this thing, right?" asked Selvi. "Are you sure she really loves you?"

"No, actually. So... what do we do now?"

"Good question," said Uncle. He rolled dice and adjusted the placement of pieces on the map. "Gwen and Cassie took out one warrior. Louis's group took out three more. The one Selvi fought has run afoul of that badger on the north end. The bug-eaters are busy with the leader — who is way above your level, before you ask. So these three are your last challenge for the night. Whatcha gonna do? Cynthia, you're up first."

"Um..." Cynthia was leafing through the cards of all her available spells. "I'm gonna use Tangle Grass on the big guy."

A die roll rattled loudly from behind the big divider. "And... wow, critical failure for the bandit," Uncle announced. "Here we go..."

The oversized bandit yelled in surprise as the grass around his feet suddenly grew long, knotting itself around his ankles. A second later, something large and heavy slammed into his gut, followed by a swift kick up between his legs.

Waving his arms in broad circles didn't help at all as he fell over, squashing the bandit mage with a loud -splat-. Grass sprang up around his wrists, his arms, his chest, holding him flat against the ground — except for the spot where the mage was poking him in the kidneys. It was only slightly less uncomfortable than the feeling of a sharpened blade being held to his neck.

"Go ahead," growled the most intimidatingly feminine voice he'd ever heard. "Try something." The rough alto seemed to be begging him to give its owner an excuse.

Not far away, a different girl's voice — a soprano, this time — shouted "*El Kabong!*" There was a dull thud, and a high-pitched squeal that he barely recognized as his older brother.

The Mistress's voice was still there in his head, but the echoes were fading away quickly. A moment later, and they were gone completely, to be replaced by shivering fear at the memory of his time with that monster. The young woman now standing with a boot on his chest and a sword at his throat was only slightly less terrifying.

If the bandit had ever been a brave man, his experiences had broken him of that habit. There was a time to stand tall and defiant, and a time to blubber like a baby.

So he did.

"Once Louis and Phil's group ganged up on the leader, it released its hold on the bandits," Uncle was saying. "None of them want to fight now. In fact, they'd probably pee themselves if Selvi said 'Boo!' loudly enough."

"Maybe I should," Shelby said approvingly.

"So, to wrap up: the bug-eaters force the leader to make an emergency exit via magic. You all stick around long enough to help them clear out the last of the workers. Louis will take care of the bandits for now, since they're victims of the ants as much as anyone, and his group's code requires them to help. You've all got your packs back, slightly singed from Bianca's fire potion but otherwise intact. The ants had a bunch of loot stored up, so you've got a fair bit of gold coming your way, plus some odds and ends that I haven't decided on yet. Most importantly, you've now got a better map of the route south. But..." Uncle pointed towards the door. "I think that will have to wait for another day."

Sometime in the last ten minutes, parents had arrived. Shelby's dad was there, bushy blond beard and all, with a slender, dark-skinned woman by his side who had exactly the same curly hair as her daughter. Mr. McCall was there for Cynthia, along with a skinny looking guy who was probably Katelyn's dad. Helen's mom was discussing the pizza fees with Max, over by the register.

"So, same time next week, ladies?" he asked.

"Yeah!" shouted Helen, Cynthia, and Claire as loud as they could. Katelyn smiled, while Shelby managed a "Sure, maybe" before getting up to join her parents.

"Enjoyed yourself after all, huh?" he heard her dad say.

"Maybe. Whatever," came the expected response.

"C'mon, Katelyn!" Cynthia said, grabbing the quiet girl by the arm. "We gotta tell our dads how awesome our princesses are!" The two of them were off like a shot.

"Thanks for doing this," said Helen's mom as she came over to claim her daughter. His niece and Claire were busy bagging dice for him.

"Not a prob, sis. They all seemed to enjoy it. Or were you all just faking, ladies?"

"It was great!" his niece declared.

"Super-fantastic, Uncle game-dude!"

He had to roll his eyes at that, but he chuckled anyway. "So, Claire. Do you need a ride home?"

"Nah, I live right around the corner. Thanks anyway."

"Will this really be turning into a regular thing?" his sister asked.

"Hope so. Everyone really did seem to have fun tonight, so why not? As long as someone's willing to spring for pizza!" He winked. It had been a good evening, for sure, and he really did hope that they'd continue on. Even the random stuff he'd thrown at the girls had turned out pretty good, and it would be fun to work with it more.

In the highest tower of the Academy, there was a room that Lady Amberyll kept to host little parties. In the center there was a low table, now heavily laden with treats. Mistress Fresnelding had made several of her favorite dishes, including a thick pie of cheese, meat, and pulped tomato baked in a cast-iron pan. Smaller bowls of fruit lay half-empty around the crumb-filled pan now, and several bottles of wine lay emptier under the table.

"Well," began Mistress Penskill as she deactivated her scrying orb. "That did not go as expected." The gnome tsked and shook her light blue head.

"But it was not a disaster, either," noted Mistress Madonnel, the teacher for the natural philosophies. "In fact, I dare say that they acquitted themselves quite well." In the chair next to her, Mistress Mehl of the training salle nodded.

"I am more worried that the Red Queen had a contingent so close to our school," said Lady Amberyll. Her green eyes narrowed. "And to send one of her own daughters with it, no less. We owe Phllthothplp and his band a debt, and not simply for aiding our students in their time of need." The ant-eater's torturous name flowed effortlessly from her lips.

"Those girls had the luck of the clouds and mountains," Mistress Heyerwif pointed out. The half-giant librarian was seated on the floor, but still towered over the rest. "They may not, the next time."

"They shall learn, and they shall live," said Amberyll. "And we shall watch. And occasionally laugh. Now," she concluded, raising her glass to the lamplight. "Do we have any more of that Kinbaresi red?"

Episode 2

"Princesses Are Never Lost"
(Everything else is simply misplaced)

It was just another sleepy summer afternoon at Max's Pizza. The last of the after-church lunch crowd had finally rolled their way out, and a much put-upon bus boy was clearing the tables. All except one, that was. Back in the far corner, a man in jeans and a comic-book t-shirt had secured a booth for himself some time before, and he obviously had no plans on moving out for the foreseeable future. There were no dishes on that red-checked cloth; the bus boy had moved them all to a neighboring table. Instead, there were half a dozen dog-eared rule-books, a laptop, several large piles of paper, and countless dice arranged in six neat groups according to color. The bus boy rolled his eyes, but left the guy alone to organize his maps and figurines. It took all kinds, and at least that was one table the teenager didn't need to worry about.

"Uncle!" a blonde girl shouted as she bounced into the restaurant. Her hair was pulled back in pigtails, and she was slightly sunburned from running around in the sun all the day before.

"Hey, Helen." Uncle sorted his papers and placed the stack on the seat beside him. "Ready for another afternoon of adventure?"

"You bet! Oh!" she cried, looking out the window. "There's Shelby!"

So there was. For a wonder, the dark-haired girl was the second to arrive that day. After all the fuss made the week before about coming at all, Uncle had wondered if she'd even show, but now she was entering the restaurant of her own volition instead of slung over her dad's shoulder. Her tightly curled hair was held back by a bright yellow band that went across her forehead and behind her ears.

"Hi, Shelby! Let's go!" His niece seemed perfectly fine with ending every sentence on a bang so far, though he wondered how long her voice would hold out. She grabbed her friend by the hand and dragged her over to the table. "It's adventure time!"

"Yeah, yeah..." The girl had her best Doubting Thomasina face on, as if the previous weekend were only a fluke, and she hadn't actually enjoyed thrashing a horde of oversized bugs.

"Well, since you're here, you can choose what you're getting as a bonus," Uncle said. "After last time, everyone definitely went up a level, which means your princess gets an extra point in the physical attribute of your choice–"

"Strength," Shelby said before he could finish.

"–and your choice of barbarian skill from this list." Uncle put the paper at her seat. "Also, as a reward for helping out with those giant ant warriors, Stu the Armadillo Man is willing to teach Selvi another skill for free."

"Stu?"

"Please, please don't ask me to try and say the name I have for him. It looks like a cat walked over my keyboard." The girls giggled at that. The previous week's adventure had included a band of bug-eating beast-men, patterned off of anteaters and other critters with more tongue than tooth in their mouth. Uncle had made all of their names intentionally impossible to say straight, and then given them stupidly ordinary nicknames like Louis, Phil, and apparently Stu as well.

"Um, what are you getting?" Shelby asked Helen.

The blonde girl plopped down on one of the booth's sofa seats and laid out her own character page. "I'm supposed to get an animal companion at level four, but I asked Uncle, and we agreed to swap it out for the level five bonus instead." She pointed out a spot that said ⌜Favored Enemy #2: Bugs.⌟

Shelby snorted, tapping the line right above it: ⌜Favored Enemy: Orcs.⌟ "So, we're gonna make 'em argue some more this time?" she asked.

"Why not? It keeps things interesting," Helen said with a wink.

The door chimes jingled again as two more girls bounced into the restaurant. Some people could be forgiven for thinking Katelyn and Cynthia were sisters, or at least cousins. They were about the same build, the same age, and had similar galaxies of freckles spread across their faces. Those people would still be completely mistaken, but it was understandable. Cynthia's red-brown hair was in its usual ponytail, while Katelyn's brown bangs kept her eyes largely hidden. A pair of doggy-ears bounced behind her.

"Hello, ladies," said Uncle. "Everyone still think last week was fun?" That got him a chorus of happy cheers plus one grudging harrumph from Shelby. "Well, today we're talking about new skills and powers. Everyone's going up a level, so you need to assign your new skill points. I wrote the numbers on post-it notes stuck to your character page."

"Awright!" Cynthia hit her seat running, sliding halfway down the sofa cushion on pure momentum alone. "Can I get the Animal Apocalypse spell yet?"

"No."

"Awww...."

"But you *do* get some neat things at level four," Uncle assured her. "Magical resistance to evil fairy-type magic –"

"Boring!"

"–and the ability to change into a wild animal once a day, for up to a couple of hours."

That got the girl's attention. He was pretty sure that Cynthia had never met an animal she didn't like. Case in point: "Oh! So I could turn into a squirrel or a raccoon or a skunk?"

"Sorry, kiddo. Too small. It's got to be something in your general size range for now."

"Giant saber-toothed squirrels?

"Nope. It also needs to be something that she's actually got some knowledge of. And since Princess Flora's fairly active but not really muscular like Selvi, she's limited to animals that average between one hundred and a hundred-fifty pounds." Cynthia was deflating like an unhappy zeppelin, so he quickly added, "I did some checking, and that would include white-tail deer, timber wolves, black bears, and mountain lions."

And there was that big, slightly buck-toothed smile, only a little feral.

"Excuse me..." Katelyn wasn't the loudest of kids, but Uncle's ears were getting used to it. "Um, I sent an email..."

"Yes, Katelyn. I got it. Okay everyone!" he said. "Claire's still not here, but we should get started. Now, Katelyn asked me if there was any way to learn the special potions and bombs that Mim used in the big bug fight last week. She can, but it requires something called multi-classing. Basically, you can choose to make your next level-up count towards a different job than the one you've got. So Princess Bianca is level four, but only the first three of those are as a Witch. The last one is also her first level as an Alchemist, which is the one that makes bombs. She meets all the requirements and has a teacher available. Everyone with me so far?"

"So we don't have to stick with just one?" Shelby asked.

"I can be a Bard, too!?" Cynthia squealed.

"Not at all, and not yet," Uncle said. "I'm gonna say here that there needs to be some logical reason for wanting to add another on, and it has to work into the game's plot. Also, you'll have to find someone willing to teach you the basics. In a town, that's easy, but out in the wilderness like you are now?" He shrugged. "Depends on who you can find and if they're skilled enough to teach. The other bug-eaters are all fighters or rangers, so if you want to try those, feel free."

"I think I'll stick with what I've got," Shelby said. Helen and Cynthia nodded.

"Okay then. Again, since you ladies are in the middle of nowhere, I have some limitations to set." Uncle counted out five red tiddlywinks disks into Katelyn's hand. "These are all the bombs you get until the next town. Use them wisely."

He dropped a green plastic disk into her hand as well. "Plus one secret potion, which Mim taught you how to make. Again, it's all you've got for now, so make it count."

-charin, charin!- The door chimes rang through the otherwise quiet restaurant. Everyone turned to look as the final member of their little group waddled in. Claire was dressed in her usual eclectic style, which today meant a jean skirt long enough to trip her, matched to a bright pink t-shirt bearing the logo of some Japanese cartoon show. No one could read it to tell just which one it might be.

"Hey, everybody! Hey, Uncle Gamer-Dude!" Claire adjusted her thick-framed glasses over her ears, and then did the same with her other pair of ears – the ones sticking out from her hairband. The hair was a dark brown. The ears were pink and fuzzy.

"Digging the kitty look," Cynthia said with a grin.

"I know, right?" Claire hopped onto the sofa next to Katelyn. "Got 'em at the mall this week... OOF!" she finished with a cry, slipping off the edge suddenly and hitting the linoleum.

"Sorry..."

"If it's a little cramped over there, you can sit by me, okay?" said Uncle. "Just no peeking behind the game master's screen."

"Why! You would impugn the dignity and honor of Her Holiness Princess Cassandrella, She who fights for Truth and Justice and the loving light of the Moon?"

"Not at all," said Uncle, rolling his eyes at the melodrama, "but I shall continue to impugn

Claire the hyperactive fan girl all I want."

"Fair enough. I promise to be good, though."

"Moving on!" Uncle said loudly over all the giggles. "Claire, like everyone else, your princess gets a bonus attribute point at level four, plus a bunch of skill points. Everybody working on those?" he asked around the table, to be answered by the frantic skritching of pencils on paper. "Good. Beyond that, she gets a few extra spells available from the Moon, and..." He handed her an index card. "A new trick."

Claire read it quickly, lips moving as she puzzled through the longer words. "Spontaneous spellcasting?" she asked.

"Yup. Remember how everyone has to choose their spells before we even start with the adventure? Well, at any time you can trade one of those spell tokens back to do one of a few things. For example, you could heal a friend, or blast a zombie with holy light."

"Smashing Moon Surprise!"

"... sure. But beyond that, you can just channel the holy energy and blast the entire area around you with either healing or evil-smiting power. And since the Moon is your patron, once you get to fifth level you can use it to dispel illusions or transformations, but that may take more power than normal to pull off." That last part wasn't actually in the rules, but Uncle felt bad about forgetting to mention this stuff the week before. And anything that distracted her from how spare the cleric level-up bonuses were was a good thing.

"Cool, thanks."

The table was quiet for a few more minutes as the girls put down skill points and chose new tricks. Uncle made the rounds, offering advice and checking numbers as they went. It didn't take too long before everything was in order. There was just one more detail that needed to be covered.

He laid a large paper on the table. On it was a three-by-three grid, with each box labeled like so:

LAWFUL GOOD	NEUTRAL GOOD	CHAOTIC GOOD
LAWFUL NEUTRAL	NEUTRAL	CHAOTIC NEUTRAL
LAWFUL EVIL	NEUTRAL EVIL	CHAOTIC EVIL

"Anyone know what alignment is?" he asked.

"Ain't that what you need when your car's wheels don't all point the right way?" Cynthia answered with another question.

Uncle rolled his eyes. "No, actually. Alignment is the game's shorthand for a character's moral compass. Is she more good or more evil? A rule-breaker or a rule-maker? That's what this grid's about. Everyone falls somewhere on here, though not always to the same degree. For example... one time I played this forest bandit, sort of a Robin Hood type who cared a lot for his people but wouldn't ever obey the king. He was definitely a chaotic good character." He tapped the upper-right square for emphasis. "His nemesis was also a very good man, but one who strongly believed in the royal right to command. That guy was on the far end of lawful good. The real villain of the story wanted to twist the laws to let himself take the throne, and so was probably lawful or neutral evil."

He took some chess pieces and positioned them on the squares. "Your character can be more on one side of a square than the other. A lawful neutral character would care about the rules above all, but could still tend a little more towards good than evil — or vice-versa. Two lawful good characters may have vastly different ideas of what that means, and even have arguments over which action is the right one."

"So why didn't we talk 'bout this last week?" Shelby demanded.

"Because I wanted you all to get a good feeling on your princesses first," he replied. "I've seen too many players who start with alignment on a character, and then not go anywhere with it. Like, making a hero who's absolutely good for the sake of good and then ignoring the reasons why, which gets boring real fast. So instead," he summed up, slipping the paper back into its folder. "I want you to keep this in mind as you play today. Is your princess more this, or that? Good, evil, lawful, chaotic, or somewhere neutral. Let me know by the end, okay?"

"Okay!" the girls chimed in chorus.

"Well then, it's time to start!" Uncle rubbed his hands together eagerly. "Anyone care to sum up last week?"

"We kicked buggy butt!"

"We decided to go on an adventure instead of staying in school all summer," Helen added.

"We fought for Love and Honor and to get our stuff back!"

"I got to do a cool magical music solo and lead an army of rabbits and squirrels!"

Katelyn just smiled. On the table in front of her was a little black stuffed cat with a red ribbon tied around its neck.

"Sounds like a good summary, ladies. Most of your rewards for this first adventure are either skills or money, because the ants had a fair store of gemstones hidden away. The biggest prize is a map of the area, which you are following now..."

Princess Gwenevrael stared at the parchment in her hands – glared at it, really, as if that would shame it into behaving properly. In her homeland, maps and charts were considered works of art, and great effort was put into making them both accurate and beautiful. So far, this one hadn't proven itself in error, but it was still the ugliest thing she'd ever seen. The cartographer should be ashamed.

"Well," she announced to the other young ladies as they finished their breakfast of fruit and dried meat. "I'd say we're either three days from the next town, or a week."

"Which is it?" Princess Selvi demanded with her usual snort of derision. "Thought you pointy-ears were supposed to know everything!"

She let the insult pass her ears without a rustle. The half-elf princess expected no less from the tusk-faced savage. "That depends on which route we take," she explained. "The road we're on now will get us there in a week, with no problems, but there's a side route that cuts right through here." She stabbed the spot with a finger.

Princess Cassandrella craned her head closer to see. The moon priestess was still chewing on a piece of the exotic, oblong, orange-colored fruit that Princess Flora's Staff of Plenty had provided that morning. "Lost Woods," she read aloud. "That doesn't sound good."

"Pffft." Obviously the barbarian princess disagreed. "It's just a name," Selvi continued. "I mean, look at the rest of it. Gloaming Canyon, Eldritch Falls, Pond of No Return... It even has a big 'Here Be Dragons' sign where our school should be!"

For a rarity, the half-elf shared the same opinion. As far as Gwenevrael was concerned, the map's sole saving grace was that it was more recent and complete than the one they'd had before. "What do you two think?" she asked the others.

Princess Flora shrugged. "It's not like we don't know our way around forests," she pointed out.

"And if anyone messes with us, then KA-BOOM!" shouted Princess Bianca. The little witch placed her cat, Jinkies, on her hovering broomstick. The diminutive black feline mewed in agreement.

"Be careful with those things," the half-elf advised. As much as the witch promised that the bundles of explosive force were perfectly safe unless activated, she still worried about putting anything that destructive in the hands of someone so... enthusiastic about things.

They made it to the woods without blowing anything up, which eased her worries a bit. The main road came fairly close to the edge of the green before forking off, but the side route was obviously the less traveled. The paving stones were broken and cracked, with weeds springing up like a green carpet leading into a palace of branches and leaves.

For the life of her, Gwenevrael couldn't see why the road was in such disrepair. Its path went clear through the woods, extending into the distance, and scores of wildflowers painted a rainbow along the ground. She figured they could get through by the end of the day, easily.

A handful of dice rattled behind Uncle's screen. It must have been a simple check, because he spoke up almost immediately: "And... you're completely lost."

"What!?" cried Shelby.

"It's not like there wasn't a clear warning on the map," he said. "Truth in advertising, ladies. As you were walking along, you paid more attention to the flowers than to the background scenery, and the path behind you sort of faded away while you were smelling the daisies."

"But Gwen and Selvi have skill points in stuff like survival," said Helen. "And tracking. And Flora's a druid; doesn't she have any tricks she can use?"

"Well?" Uncle turned to Cynthia. "Does Flora have any spells prepared that might possibly help?"

The pony-tailed girl shuffled through her cantrip cards, those simple little bits of magic for everyday use. "Yup. I figured a trick like finding north could come in handy," she said, showing him the card. "We should be settled out soon enough."

Princess Flora Fidella Del'Monica was an old hand at forests. The only thing they had more of than rocks in Silvalachia was trees, after all. Getting her bearings should've been as easy as flapjacks, but there was something funny about this place. The leaves blocked out the sun so well that it was impossible to tell where the light came from, and all attempts to climb a tree and look over the canopy got fouled by slippery bark, inconveniently spaced branches, and in one case thorns. Moss grew either on all sides of a trunk, or none of them.

In desperation, she tried an old trick of her grandfather's. She closed her eyes, placed her left pointer finger on her nose, and stretched her right hand straight out. Mumbling the magic words as she did, she should have come to a stop with her hand pointing due north after a single rotation, but it just wouldn't click for her. After spinning around in circles for a good five minutes, she was incredibly dizzy, but no closer to divining which way was north.

"Gotta be magic," she groaned as she lay on the ground. Her eyes refused to stay open until the world had settled back into place, and anyway she had such a headache coming on... "Either that, or there's no north here, which can't be right."

"Well this is a fine mess." Selvi snorted. "Any more bright ideas, pointy-ears?"

"Me? You're the one who insisted it was just a name!" Gwen shot back. "And would you look at that, we're lost in the Lost Woods!"

"Um, Gwen..." Cassie said nervously.

"And I thought all you pointy-ears were supposed to never get lost in the woods!" the half-orc retorted.

"Er, Selvi..." the moon princess tried again.

"Unlike orcish raiders who can't find their own snouts with both hands and a map!"

"What, like that worthless scribble you've been making us follow so far?"

"Must be the orcish penmanship that's making it so stupidly hard to read!"

"Will you two just be QUIET for one moment!!" All heads turned to stare at Cassie. The moon princess was red in the face, both from vocal exertion and from embarrassment. "Er, um, yeah," she added in a much quieter voice. "Were those shrubs there a moment ago?"

"What?" Even Flora was surprised by that, and she should have been the first to notice. While the argument had gone on, the forest around them had shifted yet again, with a large mass of holly suddenly springing up nearby. Her druidic senses, normally alert to the various forces of nature, were strangely muted in this place. Perhaps it was the headache, but even so she should have seen it sooner. Several trees had shifted positions, as if rotating around where they were, and the holly...

The holly was rustling and shaking without a breeze to blow it.

"That's what happens when everyone fails a perception spot check," Uncle was explaining. "Even without the penalty from headaches and arguments, only Cassandrella rolled high enough to notice something was up."

He placed a figure on the table. It looked like random bits of green sponge, cut into pieces and then reassembled with bits of toothpick. The result was roughly animal-shaped, with a head and legs, but otherwise it was hard to tell what it was supposed to be.

"So," Uncle announced. "For failing your spot checks so spectacularly, you must deal with... a shrubbery!"

There was a confused silence around the table. The way he'd said it, with a raised, nasal voice and funny accent, made it sound like he was trying for a joke. Whatever it was, it went straight over their heads.

Uncle sighed. "We should do a movie night for you ladies sometime soon. You all need to see some of the classics. Anyway, the bushes form themselves into a very large topiary animal and attack. Roll for initiative."

Five large dice rolled, and he quickly tallied up the numbers. "Okay, Flora won initiative, but she's also still too dizzy to do anything. She'll be first in line starting next round. Cassie and Bianca are tied for next up. Either of you care who goes first?"

Claire hopped up on her seat and waved her hand. "I'll roshambo you for it! Rock, paper, scissors! One, two... three!" The short girl poked two fingers into the air.

Katelyn just stared at her. Well, maybe. It

was hard to tell from behind those bangs.

"Er, well..." For once, Claire was at a loss. "Um, I'm gonna hold back, in case we need healing magic soon, and, um, I guess Katelyn goes before me?"

Princess Bianca was not having a good day. She hadn't slept well, her head was throbbing, and her stomach was taking issue with whatever that morning's fruit had been. Things had only gotten worse when they entered the forest, though she couldn't say if it was the allergies or the company that was spurring on the pain behind her forehead.

All she knew was that she was feeling cranky, and woe betide anything that got in her way. Even if that thing was a giant animated hedge that was five times her size.

The topiary beast rustled and creaked as it moved. There was nothing really animalistic about the sound; it was just the noise of wind in the trees. The thing looked kind of like a fuzzy green bear, if you squinted just right. It didn't have eyes, but it had branches sticking out like teeth and claws.

But so what? She had her magic rod. As the shrubby beast came crashing towards her, Bianca raised Gran'Mama's gift to her and let the magic fly.

"You're sure you want to do that?" Uncle asked.

"Yeah, that thing's only done weird stuff so far," Claire pointed out.

Katelyn didn't say a word, screwing up her mouth into an impatient pout and tapping the item card again.

Uncle shrugged, his shoulders rising sharply, followed by his arms and hands waving fruitlessly in the air. "Well then!" he cried. "Let's see what happens!" There was the sound of dice rattling behind the game-master's screen, and then silence. Too much silence.

"Um... Uncle?" Helen asked after a moment. "What's happening now?"

He shook his head, staring at the number he'd just rolled, and at the list of effects pinned to the divider screen. "Okay, you're not going to like this..."

Bianca's nerve was about to break. The monster was almost upon her, and her stupid magic stick was refusing to work! She shook it as hard as she could, but to no avail. The leafy green beast reared up on its hind trunks, towering above her. High, high above her... It looked like it should tower above all the trees of the forest now, but that couldn't be right, could it?

It was either that, or she was suddenly much smaller...

"Crescent Cradle Catch!" The moon princess came out of nowhere, scooping Bianca up like a rag doll and dancing away before the bushy beast could attack.

"What do you think you're doing? I had him right where I..." She trailed off as a few things became more evident to her. The leggy cleric had always been a bit taller, but now Bianca fit easily if not comfortably in her arms, with the witch's legs dangling high above the grass. Forget comparisons, she actually *was* the size of a rag doll just then. "No!!" she cried, squirming and pushing to make the cleric drop her. "Lemme go!"

She dropped to the ground with a light thud, still kicking and flailing. Not far off, she could see Gwen and Selvi as giants confronting a bushy behemoth. They... they... she was growling through her teeth. That was her fight! How was she ever going to prove herself to Gran'Mama if she couldn't beat up a dumb plant?

"We need to be careful!" Gwenevrael shouted as she and the half-orc circled around the monster. "These things are tougher than they look!" Animate topiary beasts such as this were not uncommon in the elven lands, though this was the first feral one she'd ever encountered. Much like any beast of burden, it had a vicious side that was unleashed when it lost both its fear and its respect for its handlers.

"Yeah, yeah, pointy ears. Teach your grampa how to suck eggs while you're at it." Somehow, she doubted that Selvi had ever been properly domesticated. "You take left, I take right!" the barbarian princess yelled.

Gwenevrael did as she was told, because it

was the sensible thing to do. She'd been about to suggest flanking it, herself. This way, she didn't need to argue with the khan's daughter, at least.

So she ran clockwise around the beast, slashing at it with her short sword. It made about as much difference as hacking at a real tree. A pair of pruning shears would have worked just as well, if not better. But then there was a loud rustling, a frantic fanfare of foliage that could have been likened to a growl or a roar. The body of branches and leaves tilted to the side as if pulled, but then righted itself.

"Yo, pointy-ears!" The call didn't come from the direction she was expecting. Looking up, Gwenevrael could see the half-orc's wicked grin from over the top of the bush beast. "Time to trim this thing down to size!"

With one hand gripping tightly on a bundle of branches, the khan's daughter plunged her scimitar into the beast's back. The fierce rustling announced that, whatever damage that had actually done, it was only enough to make the thing really mad.

Flora was not as on the ball as she would have liked. There was something... wrong about these woods, and it had taken her far too long to sense it. She couldn't say what 'it' was, because her head felt like it was stuffed with cotton instead of the usual grey jelly. Even now, she was still uneasy on her feet.

Communicating with the bush beast wasn't an option – even if she could speak with plants, the others had already gotten it all riled up. Her tanglegrass spell had stubbornly refused to work. The plants here simply could not block the bushy thing from moving.

That didn't leave her many choices at the moment. She could've attempted to summon help, in the form of some local beast, but she didn't. In the heat of the moment, all she could think to do was brandish her lute, shout the magic words that transformed it into a battle club, and smack that naughty, naughty plant-beast upside the head.

And all the while, she sang:

> *Whack! whack! whack!*
> *went the hammer!*

Smack! smack! smack!
went the club...

It wasn't high poetry, or even a decent effort on her part, but it helped her time her hits well enough.

Cassandrella was holding back from the action, but not once did she turn her nervous eyes away from it. She needed to be ready, she knew. Even from here, the cuts and scratches on the other princesses were obvious. The beast wasn't fast enough to get a really good hit in, but it was still dealing damage. But while she was focused intently on the fight, she was oblivious to what was going on under her nose — at least, not until the smell of strange, chemical vapors wafted past it.

"What—" Her question died in her throat as Bianca took off on her broom. The little witch clung on tight to the handle as it sped straight towards the beast. At the last moment, it zoomed upwards, and she heard a tiny voice shriek.

"Toad in the hole!"

There was a -bang-, a tiny percussive sound that was overshadowed by the roaring rustle of the bush beast. It reared up on its hind trunks, trying in vain to avoid the burst of fire that had lit up beneath it. Then it ran off, stampeding through the forest undergrowth without leaving the least trace of its passage.

Cassandrella ran over to Flora. The druid princess had been knocked over in the commotion, and was complaining loudly of a headache, but otherwise seemed fine. As for Gwen and Selvi —

They weren't there. The moon princess's eyes searched frantically, scanning the path for any sign. The two young ladies' packs were still on the ground, but that was all.

"Well now," the little witch was saying as she brought her broom back down to earth. "Toldja I could take care of it by myself." There was enough self-satisfaction in that squeaky voice to blot out the full moon. "Er, where'd the others get off to?"

"Okay..." Uncle said as he looked over the playing field. "That didn't end as expected. Gwen and Selvi were actually on top of the topiary when it bolted, so they're off on a wild ride for a bit. Looks like we're going to have to split the narrative a bit here. Which side goes first, fighters or magic-users?"

Helen and Shelby shared a look. "We'll let the magic-users go first," his niece said. "Gonna take some time to come up with a good argument."

"Take all the time you need," he said as he shuffled through his notes. There were enough encounters detailed within them for at least two or three game sessions, but they'd all been meant for a full party, not small groups. What he needed was something that the squishier princesses could reasonably survive, or at least run away from. "Okay! Think I got it straight here. Our intrepid trio of magical princesses try to follow the bush beast, but since the plants are so thick they can't get through the same way. So they strike out in the same general direction and hope for the best."

As a forest, this place made no sense, Flora had decided. Underbrush sprung up in the oddest of places, and often in the shadow of trees that should have killed off the smaller plants as a matter of course. Pines crowded together with beeches, oaks with cedar, and high grass sprung up where there should only be moss.

The path was no less a mystery, for she had no idea what had beaten the grass down to form it. Mr. Chitters had scouted in various directions and reported no sign of other animals. Brave squirrel that he was, he'd offered to go farther afield to make sure, but she'd asked him not to. Flora was afraid that if he went too far out, he'd never find his way back.

Bianca didn't have that problem with her familiar. Jinkies seemed perfectly content with riding atop all the packs now strapped to the witch's broom. The little black cat had taken one sniff at his mistress, now hardly larger than he was, and mewed with something very much like a chuckle. The witchy princess was hardly so sanguine.

"This bites frog's bottom," Bianca whined. Her legs dangled from the end of broom.

"I did warn you about using that thing," Cassie pointed out.

"Yeah, yeah." The witch waved away the words. "If that old bat hadn't given me such a dud artifact, we wouldn't be in this predicament."

"Sure..." Even the moon princess's sweet

mood had curdled a bit. Flora thought this might be the first time she'd ever heard sarcasm from the cleric.

Cassie squeaked as she tripped over something in the grass, falling flat on her face. While she picked herself up, massaging her wrists and face, there was a giggling to be heard from the broom.

Out of the corner of her eye, Flora barely caught a glimpse of Bianca's white lock of enchanted hair as it retracted. The witch was whistling and twiddling her thumbs, looking as innocent as a kid standing beside a broken cookie jar while pointing at her baby brother.

Flora's mother hadn't believed her act then, and now it was her turn to not believe it from Bianca. She should say something, she knew that, but the last thing she wanted was to make the situation worse. They'd already been split up once; she couldn't be the reason for a second time. Like it or not, the three of them had to stick together.

So she kept quiet for now, but she never took her eyes off of the little witch.

Ten minutes later, Mr. Chitters returned from his latest scouting trip full of squeaks and chirps. It was all Flora could do to keep up with him, and even so she needed him to repeat it. "There's some sort of village up ahead," she reported to the others. "At least, that's what it sounds like. A bunch of large, blocky things with doors." On her shoulder, Mr. Chitters clucked in agreement.

"Could be a cemetery," said Bianca. "Yanno, with all those big stone tombs full of ghosts and ghouls and skeletons..." The now-tiny girl's voice was as squeaky as the squirrels, even when she went "Whoooooooo..."

"S-s-stop it!" Cassie shuddered.

"Aww... is someone afraid of a few widdle ghosties and ghoulies?"

"Where!?" The cleric nearly fell over backwards trying to check every way at once, prompting more high-pitched giggles from the witch.

"It's the middle of the day," Flora pointed

out wearily. "No undead things will be out right now. We should at least give it a look."

Careful as only a druid in the forest could be, Flora crept down the path. She slipped from tree to tree, keeping hidden just in case. There was no telling what might be living in a wood like this.

Then, the village came into sight. She had to blink back surprise.

"What was that?" Cynthia asked. The pony-tailed girl obviously wasn't trusting her own ears.

"You heard me," said Uncle. "You see a circle of small houses, each about four to five feet tall, with mushroom-like roofs and walls of mud and daub. A few have chimneys, but no smoke."

"Anything else?" asked Claire.

"Well, it's very quiet," he added. "In the middle of the clearing is a spot for a fire, though it doesn't look like it's been used in a while. Flora could use a knowledge check to see if she notices anything else."

"Awright," said Cynthia, rolling her big

green die. The transparent goldenrod polyhedron wobbled a short distance, bounced off of a pencil, and came to rest with a 20 on top.

Uncle whistled in appreciation. "Okay, gimme a moment to think. What else could she notice..."

Flora grabbed Cassie and Bianca by the sleeves before they could think to approach the little village. Nestled in a clearing among the great oak trees, it was a picturesque hamlet in miniature with six identical houses set around a central fire pit.

"Huh?" Cassie had her best puzzled expression on. "What gives?"

This place was... wrong, though she'd have a hard time explaining that to the others. It was wrong in the same way that everything else had been wrong, like it'd been pieced together from someone's idea of a forest and a village without checking to see what might work. For instance...

"Those roofs... the mushrooms? Back home, we call those speckled reapers. Just touching one could kill you in a few hours. Usually they're little things, about the size of my pinky." She shivered. "They say they only grow on a murdered man's hidden grave, fed by his ghost's desire for revenge. To get that big..."

"Great, so they're bad mushrooms." Bianca rolled her eyes and made a quacky duck mouth with her right hand. "Wah, wah, wah. We still don't know who lives in them."

"Nothing good," Fiona declared.

The tiny witch shrugged. "Okay then," she said, pulling a bomb out of her pack. "Let's ring the doorbell and ask."

The round explosive was hurtling through the air before the others could stop her. It fizzed and smoked and left an impressive trail behind it before landing in the fire pit. A moment later, and a small -boom- echoed through the forest.

Six little doors popped open, and the villagers appeared. There was a baker's dozen of them, short and bare-chested with large ears and noses. Each had a cap like a mushroom's, and Flora had a hunch that they weren't the sort that you could take off. Most of the caps were a speckled white, but one was a red as dark as blood. They all had pale skin, painted blue in messy strokes, and the red-capped one sported a beard of fibrous tendrils.

Twenty-six beady black eyes stared their way, and as one the three princesses gulped hard. That was when Flora noticed that the little mushroom people were all armed with wicked-looking black knives.

"SHROOMF!" came the battle cry, high-pitched and squeaky.

Princess Cassandrella was momentarily lost in panic. What to do, what to do? The question ran through her head over and over. To either side, Flora and Bianca readied their magic, but just what could a moon princess do? Few of her spells could do damage, and those that could... she shuddered at the thought of deliberately hitting something with a face. The ants, those had been different, but these... whatever they were, they could look her in the eyes when she fought them.

The ground before them erupted into a jungle of grass and vines, all grasping and clawing at the Shroomfs. The wicked little knives went snicker-snack as they cut their way through, but the Shroomfs had definitely slowed down their advance.

Then Bianca darted forward, her hands limned with bright orange flames. The tiny witch swiped at the patch of overgrown weeds, which caught fire with surprising ease. Even this was not enough to turn back the strange little men, however, as their muttered -shroomf- could be heard not only through the burning thicket, but also to the sides. And they were getting louder.

"We need to get out of here!" Cassandrella urged the others.

"Aww, but we've got them on the run!" Bianca shouted.

"Running towards us," she corrected the witch. Several cries of "Shroomf!" punctuated her words. "We need to get out of here!" she repeated.

The magic broom could skim over obstacles like grass and brush, and Flora seemed to have no trouble with either, but for Cassandrella it was a different story. She couldn't run as fast as her long legs could manage, because she had to be careful not to trip on things. And all the while, she could hear the nasty, evil calls of the Shroomfs behind her, closer and closer.

Evil... evil... The temple elders had gone on

and on at great length about the nature of evil, though they'd never seemed to agree on much. But one thing they did say was this: evil feared the light. Sunlight, moonlight; it didn't matter as long as it was bright and pure.

Cassandrella stopped in her tracks, swinging her holy scepter of office around to face the approaching Shroomfs. There weren't quite so many of them now, after the gripping grass and fearsome flames. Blue body paint had gotten singed away, leaving tracks of dark purple and black all over their pale skin. Beady eyes followed the motion of her scepter, caught by the glittery red crystal set into the golden crescent at its tip.

The Moon shone from the heart and from the soul, she'd been taught. Cassandrella let that light shine forth now through her holy symbol. The full of the moon might not be so bright by day, but here in the shadows of the forest, it was more than enough.

Squealing and screeching, the Shroomfs all hid their eyes from the light. One by one, they slipped back the way they came.

Cassandrella watched them go, then quickly ran after the other princesses. The last thing she wanted was to get even more lost in this crazy place!

But her fears were for nothing, thank the Moon. Flora and Bianca were stopped a few yards beyond, in a little clearing by a stream. The girls' squirrel and cat were up a tree, keeping watch while their mistresses prepared for further attacks.

"They're gone," the moon princess announced as she ran up to them. "I scared away the last of them."

"What, they thought your face was that hideous?" asked Bianca.

"Huh? No, I..."

"Or was it the smell of your breath?"

"Bianca!" Flora cried. "Will you please stop it? We wouldn't even have been in that mess if it wasn't for you. What were you thinking?"

"Seriously," Cynthia said to her best friend, sitting beside her at the gaming table. "What was up with that?"

Katelyn shook her head and mumbled something. Her voice was so soft that no one could catch a single word of it, but her fingers had the tablecloth in a death pinch. Hair should not have been able to shake from nerves the way hers did.

"It's all okay," Claire said sunnily. "We made it out alive, right?"

"No," the pony-tailed girl corrected. "It's not okay. Katie, you've been actin' weird all afternoon. Dumpin' Claire off the side – yes, you did! – sayin' even less than usual, and gettin' our girls in trouble whenever possible. Do you even care about what happens?"

By now, Katelyn was practically vibrating, and tears were leaking out from behind her bangs. Uncle had no idea what the heck was going on here, though that wasn't all that unusual a circumstance.

Back behind the girls, Max caught his attention, and he nodded back to her. The tall blonde proprietor of the shop had a better head for this than he did, and if she thought they could use an early break, well... He considered the tableau before him, with two best friends in a one-sided argument about another girl, who herself looked as confused as he felt. Yeah, a break would be in order.

"It's okay, really!" the big-eyed little peacemaker kept insisting. The pink kitty ears in her headband somehow managed to wiggle in agreement. "We all have bad days. No big whup.

So let's have a nice, big hug to sort it out, and then we can have our pizza, and —"

"WILL YOU SHUT UP ALREADY?"

Uncle didn't recognize that voice, though he should have. The volume made a big difference, because he'd never heard it at that level before. Neither had anyone else, he figured. All of the girls were staring at Katelyn like she was a mouse that had just roared for the first time.

Katelyn turned bright red and, releasing her clutch from the tablecloth, ran off sobbing. The door on the ladies' restroom slammed hard behind her.

"Was it something I said?" Claire asked, puzzled.

Five minutes later, the cavalry arrived in the form of Max's special cheesy bread sticks with marinara sauce. That was more than enough for four growing girls, but the fifth was harder to entice out of her powder-room seclusion. The one time those brown bangs had found their way through the door, the eyes behind them had glared at Claire for a long moment, and then the door had slammed shut again.

For her part, the little anime fan still couldn't quite grok what was going on. She'd taken up a station by the bathroom door with a plate full of cheesy bread, and just stared quizzically.

Uncle leaned up against the doorframe and just listened for a moment. A light shuffle told his ears that Katelyn was probably right on the other side. Experience told him that the girl was probably scared out of her wits right now, too.

"So..." he began, pitching his words through the closed door. "Wanna talk?" There was another light shuffle of feet, but no answer, so he continued. "We've got time, though I can't guarantee you any cheesy sticks; at least, not for much longer. Shelby's really hoovering them up."

"Hey!" shouted the curly-haired girl from the other side of the room.

"Anyhoo, I get that you're upset and scared and all, but why not tell us what about? Couldn't hurt, might help," he finished.

A moment passed, and the door creaked a bit from the weight of a pre-teen leaning on it from the other side. "She knows what she did..." The words barely made it through the thin wooden paneling.

If "she" was supposed to mean Claire, then that certainly was not the case, because the girl in question had the look of someone desperately looking for a place to buy a clue. He put a finger to his lips to shush her before she could say anything.

It took a while to coax all the pertinent details out of the girl, and they weren't helped by the way the door muffled Katelyn's already timid vocalizations. Apparently, it all came down to last week's trip to the mall.

From Katelyn's point of view, things were simple. Three days ago, she walked out of a store at the mall, one of those little temporary places that existed only to provide ridiculously cute paraphernalia to easily excited tween girls for only a moderate mark-up. There'd been an adorable little black kitten stuffie in the bargain bin, and she was riding high on the happy vibes.

She'd spotted Claire and her cousin, who was another girl in their class, from across the way, on the other end of the bridge connecting the two sides of second-floor walking space. Katelyn had waved at them, wanting to show off her new little plush treasure.

But Claire's cousin had just pointed, right towards Katelyn, and laughed. And Claire had laughed with her.

"Wait, you were there?" Claire shouted. "Natalie was..."

The bathroom door slammed open. "Yes! I was right there!" Katelyn screamed back. "Right smack dab in the middle of the store entrance! I... I..." She coughed, deflating as she used up a whole day's worth of verbal bandwidth in one quick burst. "You... you didn't..."

Claire knelt down on the slightly greasy carpet. "I didn't even see you there, honest. Natalie and I were checking out the anime costumes, yanno? The ones in the window on the right, only they got all the wrong color wigs matched to the wrong costumes, and really, it's like they never even **watched** the show, but –"

Uncle cleared his throat. "If I may impugn your character some more, moon princess? You've got the worst poker face I have ever seen, and that includes mine. Your heart sits atop your head like neon pink kitty ears. What do you think, Katelyn? The two of you are classmates. Has Claire ever been able to hide her excitement over anything, no matter how small or insignificant or completely outside everyone else's sphere of interest?"

"...no."

"So what are the odds that she could successfully bluff her way through this conversation without it being really, really obvious that she was lying?" Uncle didn't wait for the girl to reply; Katelyn was about on the verge of tears again. "For what it's worth, think of this as a real-life spot check. You rolled high on yours and noticed Claire. She rolled low, and spotted only the biggest, brightest, shiniest, most colorful, distracting thing that her kitten-like attention span could latch onto."

"Hey! I resemble that remark!" Claire sputtered in mock-protest, which brought the ghost of a grin to Katelyn's face.

"I told you I'd be impugning you some more, kiddo. The fact remains that this is what happens when you flop your dice rolls in real life. Katelyn, did you do anything else to get Claire's attention? Wave some more, call out, jump up and down?"

The quiet girl just shook her head.

The noisy girl hugged Katelyn tight and

shook them both up from head to toe. "Wah! I'm so very very very very very very very very very very..."

"Claire, I think we get the point," said Uncle.

"SORRY!" The force of the apology actually knocked the kitty ears off of Claire's head. The two girls sat there on the floor sniffling for a moment. "Um... I saved you some cheesy bread?" she finished with a squeak.

"...thank you..." This was followed by a sniffle and a loud crunch.

Uncle walked the two of them back to the table. The pink kitty ears had changed heads, and when Claire hopped onto her seat, it was over on the opposite side from where she'd been before. He helpfully passed the girl's bag and dice over to her.

"So, shall we move on to what Gwen and Selvi are up to now?" he asked.

Cynthia's hand shot up. "Um, skyooz me, but I think we got some business to finish up here." She passed some scribbled notes over to Claire and Katelyn. "That work for you two?"

"...yes."

"Right-o-rooney!"

"Seriously! What were you thinking?" Princess Flora shouted. It was the third time she'd had to repeat the question, and it had only gotten louder in the process.

"I... I..." Bianca stuttered a bit, her eyes nervously darting left and right. To one side, there was Flora, who was looking stern and all too much like Gran'Mama before a lecture. On the other side, there was Cassie, who just looked... sad? disappointed? Whatever. It wasn't like she really cared what the little moon-bat thought about her.

Her most pressing issue of the moment was Jinkies, because he wouldn't get his fuzzy butt off of her back. He'd pounced, planted both front paws on her shoulders, and forced her to the ground before she could even react. Bianca had sent him tons of quiet, thinky thoughts, which she knew he'd heard. The little black cat had sent a mischievous chuckle the first time she'd demanded he stop squishing her, but nothing since.

"Is something wrong?" asked the moon-bat "Did we do something to make you upset?"

"Yes! Er, no? Um..." To be honest, she

wasn't sure what she was feeling that day, only that it felt like it was the whole world piling up on her, and not just a little black cat.

The fuzzbutt flicked his tail back and forth across her face, sending fur up her nose and knocking her hat loose. The floppy cone of fabric fell off completely as she sneezed.

"Um, what's that?" Flora asked.

"What's what?" she demanded back. Seriously, the druid could've been speaking squirrel for all she was getting out of this conversation.

"That." The druid reached down and poked the side of Bianca's head. Bianca felt a sharp tug that pulled deep into her skin, and she yipped in pain. "Yeah, that's really stuck in there."

"What is it? What is it?" Fear hit Bianca in one icy blast, washing away all the mean and nasty things she'd wanted to say. The pain was centered on her left temple, right above the ear.

"It's... a flower?" Flora poked it again, sounding uncertain.

Bianca was definitely certain that it hurt, and shot off a few good witchy curses that should've wilted the nearby grass and turned fuzz-butt's fur white. Neither thing happened, unfortunately. Aunt Milvy would've been so disappointed in her.

"Did you pick any flowers, earlier?" Cassie asked her.

"Yeah, right when we started walking through this stupid forest." The witch cursed again as the druid poked. "Put a pretty white one in my hair, too. What of it?"

"Well, now it's rooted in your skin, and it's bright red. I doubt that's good... Ow!" Flora yelled, yanking her hand back. "It, it bit me!"

The moon princess grabbed the druid's hand and examined it. "Yeah, that's a nasty nip. I'll have to bandage that up soon."

"What about me?" Bianca whined.

"Um..." Flora sucked on her finger and thought for a moment. "I know a spell to remove disease. That might work, but then again it might not. This thing's already well rooted, and the skin's going green around it."

"I can add some holy moon healing magic!"

Bianca was sobbing. "Please, do something!"

The druid was pulling bits of bric-a-brac

from her pocket: moss and twigs and nuts. There was no eye of newt or wart of frog in there, but then again, that was supposed to be more her thing, wasn't it? Bianca could almost chuckle at that without it hurting.

In a few minutes, they had some sort of special mud and moss packed up around her ear. The stuff covered over the flower completely, so Flora could put her hand over the spot and not get bit. The druid was droning on in that funny holy-talk of hers that no one else could understand. Bianca tried to focus on those fluid syllables and force them into some sort of sense, but they just dribbled through her mental fingers.

"O! Holy and Totally Bodacious Moon, grant unto me..." Cassie's words were no easier to understand, in spite of being in a common tongue.

There was a twinge, then a shot of bright black pain that was quickly drowned out by the light from Princess Cassandrella's holy scepter. Bianca had the most unpleasant of sensation of something moving under the skin on that side of her head, and the only positive part was that it was moving out.

A moment later, Flora pulled the entire clump of mud and moss away from her head, along with a long, string-like root that dangled limp and red. The sight of it turned Bianca's stomach, and it felt like she might—

She did. Jinkies barely got out of the way in time before she ralphed up that morning's fruit selection.

"And for good measure, you bury the bloody little flower under a big rock," Uncle concluded. "Bianca's headache quickly disappears, and she's very, very sorry for causing so much trouble, right?" Katelyn nodded. "Good, now Cynthia... you haven't been sneaking peeks at monster concepts online, have you?"

"No..." the girl sang. "Been readin' a lotta horror novels recently."

He shrugged. "Nothing wrong with that."

There was a knock on the counter behind them. Max leaned over Uncle's shoulder and picked up the now-empty plate of cheesy bread. "So, everybody okay now?" she asked, ruffling Uncle's hair into an even bigger mess.

"Yeah." "Yes, indeedy-do!" "...yes."

"Good to hear.   Anyone need more snacks?"

"We're fine, thanks," Uncle said as he passed her a ten-spot. "Could we get some pies in about an hour, though?"

Max had a hand cocked to her blonde head in a sarcastic mock salute. "Can do! Happy adventuring, y'all."

The girls all waved her goodbye, then Helen and Shelby pulled out three pages of notes and spread them out upon the table. "We're ready for our big argument now," his niece announced."

"With all that, I'd hope so." Uncle had his own notes ready on the other side of his game master's screen, complete with evil grin. "But first, you need to get yourselves out of the immediate situation."

"This is all your fault." The barbarian's tone was as blunt as a troll's club. She was brushing twigs out of her hair and grunting with each tangle.

"I fail to see how," Gwenevrael countered. "It was not my idea to ride a giant, animated hulk of shrubbery."

Selvi snorted. "Didn't take you long to follow my lead though, did it? And it was your map-readin' that got us stuck here in the first place."

"Not this again..." The half-elf shook her head. "We should find the others first, and then argue later."

"How?" Selvi demanded, waving her arms at the surrounding greenery. It was unbroken in most every direction. A monster half the size of one of her father's war elephants had crashed through just a few minutes before, but hadn't left any sign of its passage. Well, aside from its two former passengers, that was.

"It looks like there's a clearing in that direction." Princess Pointy-Ears pulled the hood of her cape over her head. "I shall go scout it and see. Wait here."

"Nuh-uh. You're not ditchin' me here that easily. We go together." Selvi struck out in the direction the half-elf indicated, hacking at the underbrush with her scimitar.

Gwenevrael sighed. "Could you be any noisier?"

"Yeah, but now ain't the time to be singin' the grand history of the clan." Selvi could hum it though. She enjoyed watching those pointy ears twitch every time she hit an odd note. Orcish ballads were meant to intimidate others in battle, so their tunes were as offensively off-key as possible. The Academy's musical instructor had given up on Selvi within the week, the khan's daughter was proud to say.

She was still humming when they reached the clearing. Then the atrocious noise got snorted all the way back up her nose and she coughed for a moment. The dim green light of the forest, filtered through branches high above, shone down upon a campsite. And not just any campsite, she noted. There was a tribal spear, its haft stuck in the ground and its point in the air. A pair of animal skulls hung from it by an old leather thong, along with a chain of colored beads and broken teeth. Selvi might not recognize the order of the pattern, but she knew an orcish camp when she saw one.

"Hey, all-yallies!" she shouted in Orcish. "Selvi Khan's-daughter of the Clan Dungivadim demands the right to hospitality for herself and her pointy-eared slave girl!" Behind her, the half-elf was protesting, but not as loudly as she might. Selvi grinned. Someone obviously couldn't speak the fierce language of warriors.

"What do you think you're doing?" Gwenevrael hissed.

"Gettin' us a bit of help," she said. "Doesn't matter how isolated they are, all orcs know my father's clan." Selvi stopped five yards from the camp and waited for the response.

No words came. Four bodies moved in the green twilight, and they certainly were orcish in shape, but they were silent. No mumbles, no grunts, and certainly no proper response to her call. They they turned to face her, and she could see why.

They had no mouths. They hardly had faces, covered by endless folds of rough, bark-like skin. Or maybe it really was bark. The same stuff covered their arms and legs, and even their armor seemed more wooden than leather.

Their weapons were wooden too, but that didn't make them any less dangerous. "Hey!" she cried, barely sidestepping the first orc's oversized club as it made its way clumsily down. Her scimitar snaked out, but before she could return the attack, a boot like a tree stump caught her in the belly.

The ranger leapt over her as she fell, with her own short sword at the ready. Much like its owner's ears, the elfy little bar of silvery metal was too pointy and not nearly as sharp as the half-elf thought. Gwenevrael stabbed at the gnarled, bark-covered face of the first orc without so much as chipping the surface.

"Well, this is another fine mess," Selvi griped as she raised her scimitar to block the next orc's unsteady blow. The only saving grace for them seemed to be that the enemy was half-blind from the disfiguring bark – the same stuff that kept the princesses' hits from doing anything. The orcs were circled around them, and even flailing blindly they could certainly hit their targets now. Selvi aimed low, hacking at ankles and feet, while Gwenevrael stabbed at where eyes should be. It was like chopping at strangely ferocious trees, and about as fruitful.

Five long notes echoed through the woods. *Du-dee-du-der-doo!* It could have been a hunting horn. The orcs all paused in place at the sound, and as one they shambled off to face the noisy newcomer.

A bush beast crashed out of the undergrowth. Unlike the previous one, this living topiary was well trimmed and graceful in its movement, and in its shape it was an odd cross between a horse and a wolf. Upon its back was the figure of a knight, kitted in full armor and his face hidden by a helmet. A heavy mace, as wooden as the orcs' own gear, smashed one of them upside the head and sent it sprawling to the ground. Greenish sap oozed from the wound.

The beast reared, clawing at the air with its front trunks, and an angry rustling filled the space between the trees. The remaining orcs grabbed their fallen comrade and hobbled away as fast as they could. The knight did not direct his steed to follow, but instead turned to face the two staring princesses.

"Be ye fair, young ladies?" The voice boomed from behind that helmet, slightly hollow in tone. Now that she had a good look, Selvi could see that the knight's entire raiment was made of sanded wood, though she didn't know what type. She wasn't a pointy-eared tree-hugger, after all.

"Fair enough," the pointy-eared tree-hugger replied. "And we thank you for your timely intervention. I fear those orcs would prove too much for us."

Selvi snorted at that. "For you, maybe. I was a single good hit away from cuttin' down one of them."

"Sure you were..."

"Don't you go doubtin' the strength of these arms," the half-orc growled. "Or I'll be showin' it to you personally."

Gwenevrael was quiet for a moment, and Selvi almost thought she'd won this argument, but when the half-elf faced her it was with clenched teeth and an angry glare. "You... you... conceited, big-toothed idiot! We are not in the eastern lands. This is not the khan's territory. You cannot just go in with your blade bared and blindly trust that everyone will be cowed into bowing down to your sorry butt!"

Oh... those were fighting words if she'd ever heard them, and Selvi already had her scimitar out. The only thing keeping the blade from separating a pointy ear from that pointy head was the knight's heavy mace, which materialized between the two princesses faster than magic.

"Ladies," the wooden voice boomed. "I know not what bad blood flows between you two, but ye shall not solve it with steel, but with words instead. Understand," he said to Selvi, "ye would not prevail against the Oaks. They have lost all semblance of thought and reflection, and barely hold to an understanding of pain and fear, little though they feel either. The forest has its roots deep in their souls. It is best if ye should quit this place ere it is too late."

"Some of us are trying, sir knight." Gwenevrael's words were for him, but her glare was only for Selvi.

"Hey, I want outta here, too!" the barbarian princess shot back. "And if we did it my way, we might be gone already. Why, my illustrious father—"

"Your illustrious father isn't here. He has no idea where you are, and frankly I can't see why he would care," Gwenevrael spat.

Selvi had always been one to prefer fists to words, so she was surprised by how much that felt like a sucker punch. There was a hollow pit in her stomach, ready and willing to devour her sinking heart. She tried to strike back, to hit Princess Pointy-Ears with even stronger words, but nothing came from her throat. From her eyes, she was surprised to feel the warmth of tears.

"Certes, ye need to talk between the two of you," said the knight. "Take this." He took a twig from his armor, snapping it off and presenting it to Gwenevrael. "So that ye may call me in time of need. I cannot linger here, and ye need your privacy."

"Th-thank you, sir knight," Gwenevrael said. Selvi managed to straighten up and nod her own thanks, though her voice still failed her.

"Well, I am off! Good luck to you, and godspeed!" The knight leapt upon his leafy steed, and the two vanished into the foliage. The two princesses stared at the shaking leaves of its wake, and then at each other.

"Talking, eh?" said Gwenevrael. "Where shall we begin?"

Princess Gwenevrael, youngest daughter of King Artundus of the Fifth Court and Duchess of the Lonely Grove, had never been so lost in her life. This wasn't even the normal sort of lost, which could be solved with a good elven-made map. Not even the greatest of cartographers could draft a chart to a person's heart, but that was exactly what she needed here.

The khan's daughter sat on the log next to her, but not beside her, if that made any sense. There was a gulf between them that was far wider than the few inches of bark and wood. She wasn't sure if they had ever had a real conversation, more than a few words, that wasn't a disagreement or argument of some sort. Back at school, they'd rarely run into each other at all, and that was only partly by accident. Surrounded by like-minded friends, neither had felt the need to bridge the divide.

Well, they needed a bridge now, and Gwenevrael could only think of one thing that would work. "I'm... sorry. I apologize for what I said. About your father."

"You mean that?" Selvi sniffled. "Not just sayin'?"

"Yes. I definitely mean it. You're not the only one who misses her father. I've barely seen mine at all in the past five years."

"Huh. That's elves for you." It was a quick, snide remark, but she could tell it was just a knee-jerk reaction.

She chose to accept it, because it was the truth. "Unfortunately yes," she agreed, which got a surprised blink out of Selvi. "I don't know how much you know of elven politics, but it is best described as the politest slaughterhouse ever conceived. The great lords and ladies live incredibly long lives, shuffling through ranks and stations on a whim, and in their boredom they find ever more creative ways to stab each other in the back. I..." She sighed sadly. "I'm a point of weakness for my father, and so he sent me away. To be safe."

"For him or for you?"

"For us. No assassins get into the Academy. I don't doubt that's why your father sent you there are well."

That bridge between them, built so far mainly on her own words, wobbled unsteadily as storm clouds formed over Selvi's face. "My father sent me away 'cause I was weak."

"Somehow I doubt that."

"What other reason is there?" Selvi shouted. "If I was stronger, I wouldn't haveta be put someplace safe. I'd be right by his side, fightin' our foes and upholdin' the Code of the Khans, like my father and his father and his grandfather the great Hamrai Khan who united the peoples of the high plains under a single banner! But no, I'm weak and my father, he... he doesn't need..." Selvi stopped herself, turning her head away so Gwenevrael couldn't see the tears she was sure were there.

Here we are, she thought as the silence deepened. *Two little girls who want their fathers to come and rescue them, though we'd never admit it*. Child of elves and child of orcs, but still the same beneath it all. She sighed and stood up. Quickly, she tugged off her right glove and presented the bare hand to the barbarian.

Selvi stared at it like she'd never seen such

a thing. Perhaps she hadn't. Gwenevrael almost always had some sort of covering on her hands, to hide the light scars that ran across the back.

"I think we got off to a bad start, back at the Academy," she said. "So let me introduce myself properly now. Hello, my name is Gwen, and I'm half human."

The khan's daughter stared another moment longer, then took that hand in her own and shook it. "Hello," she answered, a little slower and slightly confused. "My name is Selvi, and I'm half human, too."

"Well then," said Gwen, not yet letting go, "shall we two half-humans cut our way out of this gods-forsaken forest and make our fathers proud?"

Selvi grinned: a wild, sharp-toothed smile as genuine as any Gwen had seen on her face before. "Hells, yeah. Let's show 'em what princesses can do!"

"Now have them kiss and make up!" Claire exclaimed. She was jumping on her bench seat so excitedly that Uncle was afraid something would crack beneath her, or that Katelyn would get bounced straight into the ceiling.

"What?" Shelby shouted back. "Why would we..."

"Claire..." Uncle sighed and shook his head. "It's not *that* kind of role-play."

"Aw, c'mon! Yanno you wanna..." Claire had on her biggest, brightest smile, as wide as the crescent moon and even sharper on the corners. Right next to her, Katelyn was quietly giggling while Cynthia made kissy faces.

"I've got a boyfriend, yanno." Shelby glared at the three of them.

"A boyfriend we've never met," Cynthia pointed out.

"He goes to a different school!"

"Are you sure he doesn't live in Canada?" As expected, none of the girls got the joke, but Uncle felt obliged to make it. He smiled as the aroma of hot cheese and pepperoni wafted their way, and tried hard not to laugh as more than one stomach around the table gurgled loudly. "Perfect timing!" he announced. "Dinner, ladies!"

Pizza Break!

"So, um, who was your princess talkin' about earlier," Cynthia asked Shelby in-between mouthfuls. "Yanno, her great-grampa or somethin'."

The dark-curled girl took a big gulp of cola before answering. "Well, Helen and I were talking, and we thought, we're already s'posed to be thinking 'bout our princesses' personalities and stuff, so why not history, too? So like, Selvi's great-grandfather was the first Khan, and he set up all these rules so the orcs and the humans and the goblins and the whatever else in the khanate don't all kill each other. I mean, they can fight and kill each other, but in a more organized way, with rules and stuff."

"Like sports?" Claire asked.

"Awful bloody sports, but yeah," said Shelby. "Everybody plays by the Code, or they don't live long. Judges get appointed by the Khan to sorta referee, and that's what Selvi wants to do when she grows up. But she gets so frustrated cuz no one she meets on these adventures lives by the same rules, so she gets angry and hits people till they behave the way she wants 'em to."

"So where do you think she'd fall on the alignment chart?" asked Uncle. He cleaned his fingers with a wet napkin, then got out a pad and pencil to take notes for future reference.

"Well, she's big on her family's Code, and she takes promises really seriously," said Shelby. The girl fiddled with a pizza crust as she considered. "I guess most folks would call her a crazy barbarian cuz they don't get how her personal rules don't match theirs, but she'd prolly be, um... Lawful Neutral," she declared, placing her chess piece on that square.

"Sorry to tell you this, kiddo," said Uncle, "but barbarians can't be lawful."

"Says who?"

"Says the rule-book. Barbarians are supposed to be chaotic and uncivilized."

"Well, Selvi's great-grandpa was the Hamrai Khan," the curly-haired girl declared. "Named for Kublai Khan and King Hammurabi, who was the first king to create an actual set of laws, with eye for an eye and cutting the hands off shoplifters and stuff like that. Laws don't gotta be civilized. They just gotta be followed. And if people don't, then she whups 'em upside the head."

That got a chuckle out of Uncle, even as he shook his head in disbelief. "You make a compelling argument, at least. Gotta ask, though: just what are they teaching you in history class these days?"

"Only the boring stuff," Shelby said with a snort. "All dates and names, and none of the blood and guts."

"She likes to drag out her dad's popular history books for class reports," Helen added. "Mrs. Brunswick got really angry a few times, like on the report for colonial America."

"Hey, she coulda *said* that witch trials weren't an appropriate topic!"

"I think it was the historical reenactment with those old Barbie dolls..."

"Okay, I get the idea..." Uncle's sides were aching now and he was not bothering to hide it. "So, anyone else decided an alignment yet?"

Helen picked up her chess piece and placed it right on the edge of Lawful and Neutral Good.

"Gwen's been raised with a really complicated set of rules," she explained, "and she tries to ignore them as much as she can, but she's not really chaotic either. Yet."

"Do we gotta have big histories?" Cynthia asked.

"Not really, but if you want to..."

"Ooh!   Ooh!" Claire squealed. "Cassandrella's city's got a twin city on the other side of the bay – or maybe it's a small sea? – and together they worship the Moon and the Sun and..."

"And I'm going to set up a new email account for this," Uncle promised. "I'll have Helen forward it on to you all, so you can mail in your ideas and I'll see what we can work into the story. Now, Claire, what's her alignment?"

"Oh, yeah. Lawful Good!"

"No surprise there.   How about you, Katelyn?" He nodded as the quiet girl put her piece on Chaotic Neutral, but edged it up a bit towards Good. "Yeah, that fits. And you, Cynthia?"

"Lemme think... Flora is definitely a good girl, but she's really more on the side of Nature than anything else, so... Neutral Good," the pony-tailed girl declared, placing her chess piece.

Uncle made a few more notes, then clicked his pen and snapped his notebook shut. "Okay, that's all out of the way at least. Is everyone finished with their pizza?" A chorus of contented mumbles answered. "Well then, let's get things rolling. And by that, I mean use a little *deus ex machina* to get you all together again. We don't have all evening, after all."

It was easy enough for them to say they were going to cut their way out of the forest, but Selvi and Gwen were learning that words were no substitute for sharp blades. The undergrowth was stubbornly green and tough, not to mention completely annoying and inconsiderate in its lack of ears, because all of Selvi's cursing was in vain.

"Oooooh! Someone said a naughty word!"

Or at least, so it seemed at first. Selvi was about to yell at Princess Pointy-Ears for the comment when her own ears clicked with her brain and she realized that the voice hadn't sounded a thing like Gwen's. It was a lot higher, a bit squeakier, and—

And Gwen already had her sword aimed at the speaker, a little girl with light green skin and vivid purple hair that stood straight up from her skull. Two ears, pointed but not as narrow as an elf's, stuck out like diamond-shaped jug handles. She was wearing a mess of old leaves that might charitably be called clothes. The sight of a sword held right in her face got no more reaction than a curious stare.

"Who might you be?" the little green girl asked.

"My name is Gwen," said the half-elf slowly and carefully. "This is my... my friend, Selvi. And you are?"

"I'm Thistle! Are you the two who got the Oaks all riled up? Yes, yes?" she piped.

"Yes..." Gwen and Selvi shared a look. "Did the knight send you?" Gwen asked.

"Who, Sir Ulmus? Er, yes! Yes, of course!" The girl beamed. "I'm being usefully useful! Her Ladyship awaits! Mustn't keep her waiting!"

"Her Ladyship?" asked Selvi. "Is she in charge of this forest?"

The head of purple bobbed up and down, while the legs below it danced in place. "Yes, yes!

She knows every root, every tree, and every path!"

"So she knows a way outta here, then?"

Thistle paused, just for a second, before putting a finger to her chin and spinning in place. "Hmmmmmmmmmmm..." She stopped. "I suppose she does. Never wanted to leave, myself. Well! Shall we be going? Hate to leave her waiting!"

"Might as well..." Selvi said with a shrug, which Gwen mirrored. It wasn't like they had many options.

With their purple-topped guide leading the way, passage through the forest was insultingly simple. Clumps of undergrowth that would defy any number of swords parted at the touch of the girl's hand, and even heavy branches seemed to turn away. If the princesses tarried too long, then they might get a face full of foliage.

"Hope we get there soon," Selvi muttered as she picked leaves out of her hair. She had to spit a few out as well.

"Vwa-LA!" shouted Thistle, spinning on her

toes in front of a large garden gate. A thick, thorny hedge stretched either way for as long as the eye could see, with only the one break in the expanse of greenery. Unlike most everything else they'd seen in the forest, the gate was metal, with thick bars twice the height of Selvi and topped with weathered spikes. The gate itself was overgrown with delicate vines and lush flowers.

"It's certainly... welcoming?" said Gwen, noting the little wrought sculptures barely hidden beneath the leaves. Fierce animals snarled silently as pink blooms grew from their mouths.

"Yes, yes! Her Ladyship loves guests! Oh!" Thistle cheeped. "Sweetbriar! There you are!"

"Thistle!" There was an answering squeal of delight. A pink-topped girl, dressed in equally ragged leaves, danced through the underbrush to their right. The two girls met in front of the great gate, hugging and jumping enthusiastically. This newcomer's hair did not stand straight, but instead flopped down in five thick clumps resembling petals. Not far behind her, pushing through the boughs of uncooperative leaf and vine, were three other familiar faces.

"Gwen! Selvi!" Cassie waved her arms and called to them. The young priestess's dark eyes flashed as brightly as her hair when she saw them.

"Whoa, what happened to you gals?" Selvi asked when Bianca drifted into view. The witch had always been a little brat, as far as the half-orc was concerned, but now she was, well, *little*. Even that darn cat looked bigger, cuddled up against his mistress as he was. She felt a pang of worry when she saw the color of the witch's face and the plaster bandage on her head, the side of which Jinkies was stubbornly trying to bathe with his tongue.

"Don't ask," Bianca said glumly as she tried without success to fend off her familiar's ministrations. The cat let out a mewl that sounded suspiciously like a chuckle.

"Thought that stick of yours made stuff bigger?" Selvi continued.

"It does a lot of stuff, apparently. Just don't ask me what," the witch grumbled.

"I see you've got a guide, too," Gwen said quietly to Flora.

"Yeah..." the druid replied, with her own voice low. "Not sure 'bout her. Something's..."

The ranger nodded. "They seem harmless, but I'm not about to trust them just yet."

"It's not just that," said Flora. "Them, this

place, everything feels so weird. Like, it's nature, but it ain't natural, if that makes sense."

Gwen thought about the bush beasts and the orcs — or the Oaks, whatever they were called. Plants that moved, and beasts that grew bark. Thistle and her friend looked positively normal when compared to everything else she'd seen, and that by itself was suspicious, in her reckoning. "Keep your eyes and ears sharp," she whispered to the druid. "Pass the word along. We don't lie about who we are, but we don't mention the word 'princess' or anything else that makes us seem like a tempting target. We need help, but until we know what they're really up to, have your weapon ready."

Flora hugged her lute to her chest. "Gotcha."

Past the garden gates, a little path appeared beneath their feet. Pale green bricks fitted together in a complicated, blocky pattern that led them through twists and curves. Without it, Gwen realized, they would be in trouble. The garden was a maze of hedges, with splits and forks leading every which way. The two leafy girls danced straight down the brick path, however, and completely ignored all other routes. The ranger's own sense of direction gave it up as a lost cause.

After an unfortunate number of twists and turns, the green bricks ended in a little paved circle, beyond which lay the heart of the garden. There was a wide lawn, as meticulously clipped and level as in any elven citadel, with a fountain burbling at the far end. And every which way they looked, there were roses. Truly she wondered if every variety in the world might be planted here, because the fragrant blooms appeared in every color of the rainbow. Red, orange, yellow... She blinked as they passed a tiny bush with delicate petals of blue, which her father's gardeners had always insisted was impossible.

Thistle and Sweetbriar stopped in front of a circle of stone pillars. The six tall pieces of rock were ancient and dull on the edges, and might have been the remnants of an old pavilion. Or they might have have been the petrified fingers of some sleeping titan, stretching up from the depths of the earth – either seemed equally likely. The two girls never actually ceased moving, instead dancing and hopping in place with their arms carefully crossed behind their backs. As one, they bowed and announced, "We've brought your guests, Your

Ladyship!"

"Thank you, girls." That answering voice was low and sultry, sweet as the scent of roses that filled the garden. Its owner was seated on a divan, a low-backed couch with deep green upholstery that at second glance was probably moss. There was plenty of the thick green stuff arranged strategically around the pillars in a way that suggested seating cushions. Gwen had seen similar in elven lands, especially in forests inhabited by–

Dryads. That was what Thistle and Sweetbriar reminded her of. The two were strangely like the fey tree-women, and yet different. Their mistress was even more so.

'Her Ladyship' stood to receive her guests, with a willowy grace and fluidity that suggested the curve of a green branch more than the rigidity of bone. Her hair was the deep red of rose petals, hanging in a fragrant bouquet that reached down past her waist. Delicate, pale skin was tinged a light green where it was not covered by a cascade of white rose petals, somehow fixed together to provide a veil over her otherwise bare body.

"Greetings unto you," said the woman. Her smile was as red as her hair. "I am the Princess Rosalind Gracia Tatannus, formerly of Baragoccia and now caretaker of this witch's garden." Her slender arm sketched a broad arc to encompass the pillars, roses, and lawn, not caring how it pulled at her veil of rose petals. "All that ye see here is mine to care for, and in turn it cares for me. Is that not true, my little maidens?"

"Oh, your garden is wonderful, Your Ladyship!" squealed Thistle.

"Almost as wonderful as you, Your Ladyship!" added Sweetbriar.

"Ye maids flatter me," Princess Rosalind said with a satisfied smile. "Might I have the pleasure of my guests' names?" she asked.

"Gwenevrael, daughter of Artundus, lady of the Fifth Court," Gwen said with a formal bow.

"Selvi, daughter of Clan Dungivadim," her fellow half-human announced.

"Cassandrella, priestess novitiate of Selunika!"

"Flora Fidella DelMonica, of the united clans of Silvalachia," the druid said simply. She nudged the little witch beside her.

"Oof! Um, Princess Bianca of the Western Winkwoods," the witch said, not seeing the collective wince of her fellow young ladies.

"A princess?" Rosalind said with glee. "Oh, this is an occasion indeed! It has been so long since we have had the chance to entertain fellow royalty. Though thou art quite small for a lady of such high stature."

"I've been ill lately," Bianca said. "Fragile disposition and all that." She sniffed derisively. "Hard to find proper food on these long voyages, you know."

"That I understand," their hostess said. "Come, come. Sit a while. Thistle, Sweetbriar, fetch some water and fruits for our guests!"

"Yes, Your Ladyship!" The two girls scampered off, returning only a few minutes later with a large pitcher of cool, clean water and a basket filled with assorted fruits. There were apples and cherries, oranges and berries, and a few that even Flora couldn't identify for sure. As the princesses settled on their mossy mats, they could all agree it was a pleasant welcome.

"So how did you come to this place, Your Highness?" asked Gwen. "You said you were from... er..."

"Baragoccia, wasn't it?" Bianca piped up. "I've heard of that place, somewhere. Maybe in a book, hmm..." The little witch pondered as she bit into peach nearly the size of her own head.

"Oh! it is a sad story!" said Thistle.

"Very, very sad," agreed Sweetbriar. "Please tell them, Your Ladyship!"

"We don't mean to pry," said Flora hastily.

Their hostess shook her head, sending loose rose petals to drift off her shoulders, and gifted them with another radiant smile. "It is not a bother. I enjoy having new audiences to play for. Let me begin, then." With a snap of her fingers, a harp materialized out of the ground, like a tree for which years passed like seconds. Fan-shaped leaves spread out from its trunk, and wiry vines became strings to be plucked by Rosalind's fingers.

"It all began on the happiest day of my life," she sang as she played. "My wedding to Prince Marti of Carpazha. It was an event of such beauty, and we loved each other so very much. But then she appeared." The strings cried out in pain as she dragged her nails upon them. "A witch, old and ugly, who hated me so for my youth and beauty."

"What was her name?" asked Bianca, somehow missing the furtive but frantic signs from the others that she should be quiet.

"She called herself Alvatra," said Rosalind. "Why do you ask?"

"Um, no reason," said Bianca, who'd apparently just realized that it wouldn't be wise to identify herself as a witch. "Thought that if she was so famous, I might've heard of her before. Sorry to interrupt."

Rosalind needed no apology, nor permission, to pull another long and complicated string of notes from her harp strings. The interlude continued for many minutes before her voice rose once more into song: "Alas, my wedding was ruined on that day, for the witch Alvatra came to steal me away, to this garden to be its warden, and since that day I have stayed. Dark magics she wrought, so that all who sought me would know me not. A rose was my name, and so I became the centerpiece of her garden."

"What terrible tragedy!" cried Thistle.

"What tragic terror!" squealed Sweetbriar.

Their lady nodded, and they accepted the touch of her slender hand like it was the caress of an angel. "There, there," she cooed at them. "One day soon, my dear Marti will come, for he promised to rescue me, cried it for all to hear as that witch pulled me from his strong arms."

"Um, how long have you been here?" asked Flora.

"Not so long as one would think," Rosalind assured. "This is a feywood, stolen by the witch from its original masters long ago. Time runs faster here, so a few years may only be a matter of weeks to my Marti. He will come."

"But..." Bianca's voice quivered through the still forest air. "The kingdom of Baragoccia was destroyed over a hundred years ago, in the Palachkit Wars. I just remembered..."

The harp strings screamed as Rosalind clawed at them. "Thou dost lie!" Her voice matched her music in tone, and the green light of the grove flickered as it passed over her body. A cloud seemed to shroud the sun, leaving them all in a shadow lit only by the bright petals of the roses. Princess Rosalind's eyes glowed brightest, in a deep bloody scarlet.

"You just had to blurt that out," groused Shelby as she watched Uncle swap out the three neutral character pieces for hostile ones. "Seriously, did we need to have all those wisdom checks? We know better than to blab like that."

"Sure you do," said Uncle. "Because you know that this is a game. But they don't." He quickly tidied up the princess pieces on the board. "Just as they couldn't realize that Rosalind's harp music was making it progressively harder not to just sit there and appreciate her beauty — which is why you're all going to need to roll better than a 15 to break the effect. Ready, ladies? Time to roll 'em!"

Five large, colorful dice rolled — and they rolled surprisingly high, Uncle was annoyed to note. Even before counting in all the bonuses, three of the princesses were over the needed number. After everything was added in, Selvi and Flora actually cleared the 20 mark.

"Sorry, Claire," he said after the final tally. "Princess Cassie is still starstruck. Everyone else, on the other hand..."

Selvi Khan's-daughter had been on edge for the entire performance. Gwen and Flora had both quietly warned her to be on guard, but their words weren't necessary. Something was so obviously wrong with the situation, and it wasn't just the way the harp strings hurt her ears with their sharp-edged twang.

So when their hostess began ranting and raving, Selvi took it for the opportunity it was, and lunged straight for the flowery princess. She actually managed to get a hand around that delicate, arching throat, only to be met with pain.

Her battle cry curdled into a whimper of shock as a dozen thorny spikes shot through the meat of her hand. When she fell back, Selvi could see a dark necklace of blood – her blood! – circling Rosalind's neck. The flower princess's smile pulled back to reveal a row of fangs to match the scores of thorns erupting from her skin. With one delicately clawed finger, Rosalind wiped a crimson droplet from her neck and licked it.

"What a curious flavor," was all she said, and then she was gone.

Gwenevrael had been just a beat behind Selvi, and caught the khan's daughter as she collapsed. The ranger did not envy her the glory of going first; it looked far too painful. Her sword was bared and ready to slash, but Princess Rosalind was nowhere in sight.

"Tut-tut," echoed that silky sweet voice,

somewhere in the gloomy distance. Dryads, the half-elven princess now remembered, could magically jump to their soul tree at any time. "What ill-mannered guests! Thistle, Sweetbriar? Would ye maidens please show them the error of their ways?"

"As you wish, Your Ladyship!"

"At once, Your Ladyship!"

Their two guides were still perched on a nearby rock, not too different from how they'd been scant moments before. They were no taller, no stronger, but their body language had changed completely. Feet no longer danced in place; instead the girls crouched, and their outlines in this unnatural dusk seemed much jagged than before.

That momentary glimpse was all the warning any of them had.

Flora barely managed to jump out of the way in time, and she could feel the fabric of her blouse catch on Thistle's spiked arm. The purple-haired girl pulled, knocking the druid off-balance. One skinny leg snaked around to sweep Flora's feet out from under her, and then she was on the ground with a walking weed standing on her chest. The little girl was not nearly so cute now, with her thorns exposed and her teeth all sharp. One prickly fist rose up, and Flora braced for a punch—

Which never came. Instead, a tiny, squeaky voice shouted "Head's up!" and then a magic broomstick collided with Thistle. Bianca clung defiantly to the length of elm wood as it slammed repeatedly into its target.

Flora rolled over and bounced to her feet. On her left, the little witch led an irate Thistle on a wild goose chase, while on her right Gwen fended off Sweetbriar. Selvi seemed to be hurt, but Cassie... The moon princess was still sitting there with glazed eyes and a simple grin plastered on her face. Over, around, and throughout the little scene, the sound of Rosalind's harp wrapped itself, at times beguiling and at others screeching.

"Oh no she ain't," the druid muttered. She'd hung around her Uncle Alvis enough to recognize the influence of bard song. Even though she knew what it was doing, she couldn't quite shrug off the tune's insidious whisper, that little ringing in the ears that said "Give up; there's no point..."

Well, like grandpa'd once told her,

sometimes you had to fight fire with fire. The elder druid had meant it as a lesson in keeping forest fires from spreading, but she figgered it applied here, too. Bringing her trusty lute to bear, she called up the memory of a favorite tune from her Uncle Alvis and made up the words as she went along:

> *Y'ain't nothin' but an old bloom,*
> *withered on the vine!*
> *And as for your old thorns,*
> *oh, pay 'em no mind!*
> *Cuz your withered old thorns,*
> *oh, ain't no threat o' mine!*

She played and sang as loudly as she could, hoping for the best. For a moment, it even felt like she was getting somewhere, pushing against the tide of depressing harp music. There was a lull in Rosalind's rhythm, a pause, and then:

"A fair try, girl, but a bard thou art not." Then the shrill cacophony of harp-strings began again.

With a start, Cassie remembered to breathe. Her head felt like it was stuffed with soft bunny fur, and she almost fell over when she tried to stand. All around her, the other princesses were fighting. Well, most of them at least. Not far away, Selvi was also on the ground, curled up and cradling her left hand.

"Er, hey. Um, you okay?" She rolled over to the half-orc, not yet trusting her sleepy feet. The only response she got was a harsh growl. "Okay, not good. Me neither," she babbled. The wool in her head was slowly clearing away, but it was scratchy and itchy as it went. "Er, um, let me..."

Somehow she held her holy scepter steady, keeping it level between them. As quickly as she piously could, Cassandrella intoned the holy words, finishing with a simple "Moonlight Mercy!" Soft, comforting light surrounded the two of them, stripping away the last of the bunny wool. Selvi seemed to be doing better, too.

"Thanks." The barbarian princess still winced as she flexed her left hand, but she was up and ready. "Time to chop that rosy bi... bush," she corrected herself under Cassie's sadly disapproving gaze. With a wild howl, Selvi ran off, brandishing her scimitar.

The moon princess shrugged and looked around for more friends to help. She didn't notice anyone in dire need, but she could see one thing for sure: rippling spots in the hedge surrounding the grove, where leafy green lupine forms slipped in.

"More monsters!?" Shelby was going cross-eyed at this point, trying to send death-stares at Uncle. He just laughed.

"The children of the brush, what quiet sounds they make," he said, sure that after all the other missed references, none of the girls would get this one.

"Ooh, is that s'posed to be a *Dracula* joke?" Cynthia asked. "So, is Rosalind like a vampire or somethin'?"

"...or something," he admitted. The villain of the piece had been quilted out of bits and pieces, but some elements of the vampire template had been included. "Good guess."

The pony-tailed animal lover preened at the compliment. "Okay, got a question for ya," she asked, pulling out her spell cards. "Got a level-2 magic here that changes the size of animals, but it just says they get smaller. Can I make something bigger?"

"Afraid not," he said. "That's a different spell entirely. A level-5 one."

"So Flora can use it pretty soon?" Cynthia asked hopefully.

"Nope. She won't have fifth-level spells until level nine." That got him a full set of deadpan stares from around the table. "Hey, don't blame me for how the game's set up. I'll freely admit that it can be a bit confusing, but that's the way it is, and the spell to make animals bigger is way above Flora's ability."

"But she could do it to people!" Cynthia cried, pointing at Katelyn. "She did it last week!"

"...the staff did it..."

"Yeah, but I bet Bianca could learn how to do it herself, right?" Cynthia had her game face on now, all pouting lip and glaring eyes. "What level of spell is it, to make people bigger?"

Uncle hated to concede the point, but... "For wizards and witches, it's a level-1 spell," he admitted through clenched teeth.

"How does that even make sense!?" Cynthia shouted. "People are just animals with more clothes on! And the clothing changes size too, I bet. That's gotta be harder than making Fido and his collar bigger! Why do wizards and witches get one set of rules, and druids another? What's fair about that?"

On the far side of the table, Helen and Shelby had procured a large piece of scratch paper and a marker, and quick as a wink they'd made their own protest sign: EQUAL RITES FOR DRUIDS! Soon enough, the entire table was chanting "Equal rites! Equal rites!" Even Katelyn managed to be heard.

Uncle felt a headache coming on, and he didn't have any aspirin. He did have dice, though. "Alright, alright. One roll, no bonuses, difficulty check of 15. You want it, this is your only chance."

Cynthia narrowed her eyes and grabbed her twenty-sided, the goldenrod one. She blew on it twice for luck, rolled, and sent it clattering across the table. -gatta, gatta, gatta- it went, bumping and jumping until it stopped at... 17. There was cheering all around.

"Okay," Uncle said with a sigh. "So now your level-2 size-changing spell can work in either direction. At the time of casting, you can choose to make the target bigger or smaller, but you still only get to use it once a day and it won't last too long. Dare I ask what you plan to do with it?"

Two of the hedge-wolves had split off from the pack to stalk Flora, but they didn't immediately attack. They circled her, wary of the oversized club she was waving their direction, looking for a weak spot. They'd find it soon, she figgered. That was the way of the wild; there was always something that could eat you, no matter how strong you were. But what would eat a wolf made of foliage...

"Mr. Chitters?" she called. The squirrel bounded up her shoulder. "Do you trust me?" There was an affirmative squeak in her ear. "Okay..."

The magic words were short and simple. Druidic wasn't a very complicated language, for those who could speak it. In fact, all she had to do was change one accent point from down to up, and then—

There was a swirl of green light from her shoulder, and a sudden weight that got bigger even as it leapt from her to the space in front of the approaching wolves. Mr. Chitters let out one long chirp that got louder and deeper as it dragged on: Squeeeeeeeeeeeeeeeeeeeeeeeeeeeeeeeeeeeeeeeeeeaaaaaaa

aaaaaaakkkkkkkkkkkk!

And suddenly the hedge-wolves had a new problem: an angry, bushy beast larger than they, with very sharp front teeth and an appetite for greenery. Mr. Chitters pounced, going straight for the nuts and berries as only a true squirrel could.

Bianca wooshed around the battle, trying hard to keep track of everything. On her left, Selvi was chopping at hedge-wolves with wild abandon, while on her right Gwen was defending Cassie from the pink-haired Sweetbriar, now all prickly and mean. Beyond them, she could see Flora as the druid commanded her squirrel to attack, and then joined the battle herself in the form of a small bear.

The little witch was impressed, and somewhat disheartened. Much as she hated it, she was still two sizes too small to do anything more than annoy people. But... she grinned as she pulled the broom around. The purple-haired Thistle and a gang of leafy beasts had rallied to make a rush at Selvi, and so gleefully did Bianca sweep over their heads. Jinkies hissed loud, nasty things from his perch, in those tones which cats reserve for cussing. And of all the languages of the beasts, feline really was the best for that sort of thing.

It certainly got their attention. Bianca kept the broom to about head-height, going slowly enough for the hedge-wolves to keep up, but swift enough that they'd never catch her.

"Not so fast, my dear." And suddenly Princess Rosalind was there, rising up from the nearest rosebush like a particularly tattered flower. Rows of thorns lined her mouth instead of teeth, now that the magic of her glamour was off, and trickles of reddish sap leaked from the petals around her eyes. Bianca had to spin and twirl to avoid running into the rose princess's prickly embrace.

"Let us leave this forest, or you'll be sorry," she warned in her most imperious and princess-like tones. The effect was marred by the high-pitched squeakiness of her voice, but she thought she did pretty well.

"I think not." A long, twisted tendril sprouted from Rosalind's arm, and with a flick of the wrist she snapped it at the flying broomstick. Bianca cried out as the thorns scraped across her leg. "It has been so long since I have entertained guests, and yet Alvatra's curse still holds me. None who enter this grove may leave alive." A green tongue ran over those thorny fangs. "And I admit, I could do with a bit of... watering. Do not worry; it will only hurt for a moment, and then thou may'st join Thistle and Sweetbriar as my newest handmaiden. And then we shall enjoy all our days here so greatly. Soundest that not like heaven?"

"Um, let me think... no. In fact, let me answer that emphatically." She palmed one of her three remaining bombs from the inside pocket of her gown. "Hells no!" she shouted, throwing the miniature incendiary straight at the rose princess's feet.

Rosalind vanished with a shriek, but the bush wasn't so lucky. It burst into flames reminiscent of the candles on Gran'Mama's last birthday cake, only no one was handy with a spell of extinguishment to put this one out.

"Thou art a little beast..." Rosalind angrily sputtered, stepping out of a rosebush some ten feet away. "Princesses should not behave in such a manner!"

"Oh, shouldn't we?" Bianca asked slyly as she glanced around the grove. "Get with the times, Rosie. We're princesses, and we do whatever we want." She pegged the next rosebush with a bomb, and then one more for good measure.

Rosalind was screaming bloody murder, but the little witch was just getting started.

With her free hand, she drew a small but complicated sigil on her throat. A second later, the spell was active, and her next few words exploded out with enough force to strip the leaves off the nearest hedge-wolf: "AIM FOR THE ROSE BUSHES, EVERYONE!" To her amazement, everyone actually listened. Selvi and Gwen turned their swords on the plants, severing them at the base with powerful chops. The bear that was Flora ripped a few more out of the ground, while her oversized squirrel put its oversized incisors to good use. Cassandrella, lacking in the sharp implements department, stood back and cheered the others on.

"No!" cried Rosalind, jumping from bush to bush. "Not... not the... must be protected..." The rose princess's voice faltered and weakened with each bush lost.

Bianca was regretting that she'd wasted those two bombs earlier in the day, and that she'd neglected to prepare more than the single fire spell either. But on the other hand, who needed that when you had a magic rod of... whatever it was it did? The Rod of Random, she'd decided to name it, though at the moment it was practically a staff as far as she was concerned. Bianca took aim at

Rosalind, invoked the rod's power, and waited to see what happened next.

A bright flash burned through the space between them, accompanied by a crack of thunder so strong it knocked her from the broom. A single bolt of lightning cut through the air, leaving a bright black scar in its wake. Rosalind caught the worse end of it by far. At her feet, the large rose bush burst into flames, and this time the flower princess was too stunned to jump away. Hot, red fingers burned their way up her body, scorching through the thin, petal-like material of her garments with a flash, leaving only bare skin now blackened and charred.

The strength of her screams lasted for many long moments, pushing all other sound out of the grove, and in their wake was a dull, heavy silence. The remaining hedge-wolves fled as quietly as they'd arrived, while the girls Thistle and Sweetbriar knelt sobbing on the grass.

It was a long moment before any noise dared break that silence, and when that twig snapped under the purposeful step of a boot, everyone turned to look. The knight in wooden armor, Sir Ulmus, approached with no other sound to herald him. Leaving his mace on the trampled grass, he knelt by the scorched and ruined body of Rosalind.

"Where..." The words were hardly there, light as a forest breeze. "Where wert... thou... madest... a vow..."

"Yes, my dearest, my fairest Rose. I promised to protect thee, all those years ago, longer than the witch's curse could let thee remember. And yet, never could I protect thee from thine own actions." He held her body close for another long moment, until it hung limp and lifeless in his arms. Then he laid her back upon the ashes. "Perhaps now thou shalt know peace."

"We... we're sorry, sir knight," Gwen said. "We never intended..."

"Well do I know the truth of thine words, elf-maiden. Ye ladies were victims of this place and its glamours, and Rose, dearest Rose... She had no choice, ye must understand. Once ye were here in the garden, it was certain that she would attack eventually. Such was the nature of her bindings."

"Sir Ulmus! Sir Ulmus!" Thistle and Sweetbriar cried, rushing to the knight. "What is going on? Our heads hurt so..." Clear sap was running from their eyes.

"The roots of the lady's influence have left your minds," he explained, "and ye are as free as ye have ever been. Would that I could restore to you your lives of old, but alas, I fear those are centuries lost." He patted the girls tenderly on their heads. "Let me be a father to you, at the least, that ye might know better in your new lives."

"I'm sorry!" It had just hit home to Bianca that there was a body, smoldering on the ground, and that she'd put it there. "I... I shouldn't have... could have..." She ran up and hugged the two green girls, ignoring the slight prickles that still covered them.

"Um, if we ain't a-fighting now," said Selvi, "could we get an explanation or something?"

"Ah, yes." The knight nodded. Reaching up, he twisted and pulled at his helmet until it was free in his arms. The face beneath it was remarkably human, if one overlooked the greenish pallor and the mossy beard. "Glad am I that thou didst not require the token of my aid, maiden elf. If thou hadst called me, I know not how my loyalties would lie. We are all victims here, though none as tragic as poor Rose herself." He sighed. "Let us move away from here a ways and discuss."

The princesses followed him back towards the pillars. Gwen pulled a spare cloak from her bag, still propped against one stone, and returned to Rosalind's side to drape it over the body. Everyone pretended not to notice how she double-checked the fatal circumstances of the deceased before joining them.

"I presume that Rose did tell you the story of how she came here?" The princesses nodded. "And I am sure she did not start it proper, for it began not at the wedding, as she so often claims. Perhaps she remembered not, but it was in fact three days before that event, during the celebrations of betrothal. As per our custom, she and I traveled the lands around Carpazha, handing out small coins to all whom we met. On her journey back to the castle, she met an old crone who asked for a scrap of food or other such kindness. Rose was always too clever for her own good, and played the old woman, presenting her with a piece of gold, only to exchange it for a brass disk by sleight of hand."

"Um, was she stupid?" Selvi blurted out. "I mean, that's the kinda story they teach in basic princessing class. No way that old lady wasn't some witch or fairy or something."

"Certes, we realized that soon enough, but witches were new and strange things to us, to be found only in far-off lands. Alvatra Hag's-daughter was the first to come this far north."

"Hag... this must have been seven hundred years ago, at the least!" Bianca cried from within Thistle and Sweetbriar's sniffly snuggles. "None of the original hag-daughters are still alive!"

"I cannot vouch for thy words, young miss, though I doubt them not. Rose would claim that time flowed oddly here, but in truth I believe that was merely another sign of the malaise of her mind. She never stopped waiting for her prince to come and rescue her, though it was long ago that I led an army against Alvatra," the knight continued, "up to the castle which once stood at the heart of this wood. It was my sword which slew the witch, and I found my dearest Rose in this very garden..."

"And she killed you," Flora guessed.

"She did what was now her nature," the knight replied. "Dark magics were worked upon her, and Rose was no longer the same, and would not regain her senses for many years after. She never knew that her Marti died that day, to be replaced with Sir Ulmus, her trusted defender. Occasionally others would happen upon this place, to be devoured and perhaps converted into her slaves." He nodded at Thistle and Sweetbriar, huddled into a sobbing clump around the diminutive Bianca. The little witch had the most conflicted and perplexed look on her face.

"Okay, this answers the what and the why," said Gwen. "Now for the how. As in, how do we get out of here?"

"That I can answer," said Sir Ulmus. "At the far end of this garden is a gate of stone. Through it one can go many ways, but I only know of certainty the one which leads to Carpazha. Would that suit you ladies?"

Selvi and Gwen shared a look. "If it gets us out of this forest..." the half-elf began.

"And farther from school!" the half-orc added.

"...then I think that shall suffice," Gwen finished.

"And so," Uncle concluded, "after some more talk with Sir Ulmus and some consolation to the two flower children, you make your way out of the Lost Woods once and for all. Hopefully we figure out where you are by next week."

"Finally!" shouted Shelby. "Worst shortcut ever!"

"Well, pay attention to the map next time," he teased back. "Time to tidy up, ladies. Remember to mail me back with your plot ideas for upcoming adventures..." He scooped up the small pile of sticky notes that was gathered at Katelyn's place at the table. "I've been giving you prompts; now it's time for you all to return the favor."

"Roger that, Uncle Gamer-Dude!"

He was all ready to impugn Claire some more, just on general principle, when Uncle realized that they now had an audience. The evening crowds had slowly rolled in, and not far from their table a family had been seated. A raven-haired girl in a blue one-piece was staring at them.

"Claire? Is that you over there?" the girl called. "And Helen! Shelby! Hello!" Now she was waving.

"Hello, Natalie..." his girls sighed in chorus.

"Ooh, is this what you were talking about doing on the weekends, Claire?" The alleged Natalie hopped on over. "Can I try?"

"Didn't think it'd be your thing," Shelby said. "It gets really complicated."

"Oh, if Cynthia can do it, I'm sure I can manage. How hard can it be?"

The pony-tailed girl held her tongue, though Uncle couldn't miss how Helen and Katelyn both had their arms locked around hers. "Excuse me," he interrupted. "How do you know everyone?"

"Oh, I'm Claire's cousin Natalie. We're all in the same class at school. Hey, can I play next week too, please?"

"Honey," Natalie's dad said, coming up behind her. "Let's not bother people..."

"It's not like they're strangers, daddy. It's Claire! And the others are my friends from school! Right?" Natalie said, to be answered by noncommittal nods and grunts. "See! So is there room for one more?"

"I don't know," said Uncle. "What do you ladies say?"

Cynthia and Shelby looked like they'd been sucking lemons, but of the five only Claire spoke up: "Sure, we can give it a try." She gulped at the end, skewered by four other sets of eyes. "I mean, it's all about playing around and working together, right? The more the merrier?"

"Perfect!" said Natalie, grabbing Claire's hand and giving it a shake. "Oh, this is going to be awesome!"

"You'll still need to draw up a character," said Uncle. "Do you know how, or should I arrange something?"

"Oh, I'll just get my big brother to help. He

plays this kind of game all the time. Hey, Kyle!" she shouted to the young man at her table, who'd been studiously focused on his pizza. "Can you make me something this week?"

"Mmrphlhmf?"

Uncle jotted down his email and passed it to Natalie's father. "Have him get in touch with me, and we'll hammer something out."

"Sorry to impose like this," her father replied.

That got a shrug. "Two things this game is good for," said Uncle. "Making friends and making enemies. Hopefully this will be a good experience all around. Right, ladies?"

"Yeah." "Maybe." "Sure it will!" "...hope so..." Cynthia abstained from the chorus and quietly fumed in her corner.

He tried not to sigh. This idea reeked like an Easter egg at Thanksgiving, but then again, he'd made friends around the gaming table after far less auspicious introductions. Maybe Helen could give him some insights into the situation later, but for now, as the girls gathered their things and went home with the parental units, all he could do was try and figure out how to best fit this newcomer into the story...

The scrying room, high up in the west tower of Lady Amberyll's Academy for Young Ladies, was a wide, airy chamber that was nevertheless as cluttered as a magpie's nest. The many and varied instruments of divination were present: the viewing pool, the crystal balls and enchanted mirrors, the arcane cards and sacred dice, all strewn across the broad table. Everything had seen plenty of use that day.

"Well, they're safe," Mistress Penskill announced with a groan. A full day's frantic work, and that was about all she could say. The Academy's head instructor of the mystic arts had had better days. First, the magical automata she'd set on the scrying pool had sent the alarm, alerting her too early in the day that something had happened to those girls she needed to watch over, and then... nothing all day. The girls were gone, vanished, and nothing could tell her why or how. No spell at her disposal could find them, and Freja Heyerwif was away doing librarian things, so there was no one available with better. The blessed situation was enough to make her want to pull her hair out!

"You worried too much," came headmistress's reply. Lady Amberyll was seated a safe distance away, on the seats meant for the audience so as not to disturb the diviners at work. Mistress Penskill would rather she not be there. "All's well that ends well, Penelope."

"My lady!" she shouted back. "Five of our pupils vanish for an entire day, only to reappear injured, and... and... whatever it was that happened to Bianca, and that's *all* you can say?" The gnomish magician huffed and smoothed down her blue hair. "They could have died in there, and we'd never know!"

"But they didn't."

"And we can't even tell how they suddenly jumped two hundred miles to the east!"

"No, but I am sure we can find out."

Damn the woman! Mistress Penskill could feel her hair going straight up again, powered by her anger and frustration. "My lady, I must protest! This was supposed to be an educational adventure for them!"

"There is no education without risk, Penelope dear. And we cannot hold their hands or dictate just what dangers they face." In contrast, the lady's silvery hair was perfectly in place, unmussed by any emotion.

"Reckless, that's what it is! Reckless and dangerous and ill thought-out!" Mistress Penskill hopped onto a stool just so she could look the headmistress right in her emerald green eyes. "And I'm through with it," she announced. "These girls need help, need some protection, and I've already contacted the Temple of the Sun and Moon closest to their current location. They are sending someone to escort the girls to safety."

"You will do as you see fit." Lady Amberyll's lips quirked, almost to form a smile. "That is why I took you on as an instructor, as I recall. I have no problem with it. I hope only that it turns out for the best."

"Anything is better than a dead kid on my watch."

Now Lady Amberyll sighed. "Trust me, Penelope, when I say that yes, there are worse things that could transpire. Worse things that *will* happen, in time. Early trials shall bring them together," she said. In the far mirror, the princesses Gwenevrael and Selvi Khan's-daughter were talking and laughing. It was not a scene that anyone at the Academy would have recognized. "Yes, it is risky, perhaps even reckless, but it may well be worth it in the end."

Episode 3:

"Princesses Don't Play Nice"

Sunday luncheons were always the busiest time of the week at Max's Pizza, as station wagons and mini-vans clogged the parking lot while their passengers filled the seats. But like any force of nature, this tide of humanity withdrew almost as swiftly as it crashed in, leaving behind a strand line of crumbs and crusts. In the back corner, one table was close to pristine, if only because its occupant had bribed the busboy to take care of it first. What it lacked in grease puddles and burned crunchy bits, it made up for in clutter. There was a heavy stack of dog-eared books holding down one corner of the tablecloth, and a small laptop computer sitting on the next. Several large posters lay rolled up under the table, while on top of it was the map of a town, along with a mismatched assortment of figurines and game pieces that had long since outlived their original purpose.

It was the figurines that first roped in the attention of the five-year-old whose family was just now finishing lunch, but the dice were what really kept her there. The brightly colored plastic polyhedrons came in every shade of a particularly psychedelic rainbow, and were nothing like the inquisitive little girl had ever seen. Her parents had tried to pull her away once already, but the blonde girl in the white one-piece who was stationed at the table had reassured them that little Cecelia wasn't getting in the way. In fact, CeCe was more than happy to help the older girl as she sorted the dice into various color groups, and waddled off a few minutes later, satisfied in the knowledge that she'd been helpful.

"I see you made a new friend," Uncle noted as he returned from the toilet. Helen just smiled as she quickly rearranged the dice into their actual, proper piles. "Should we add another chair to the table, you think?"

Helen giggled. "We might have to wait a few years until CeCe knows her times tables," she said. "Still, she'd be more fun than Natalie coming in."

"Seriously, is the girl that bad?" He had to ask. Helen's classmate had pushed her way into joining the game last week, and he still wasn't sure if it would have been better to just say no. The ever-positive Claire had spoken up for her cousin, said to give her a go, and the other girls had grudgingly acquiesced, but Uncle was afraid that 'grudge' would be the operative word here.

Helen's friend Shelby shared a lot with her barbarian princess avatar, especially in the temper department.

"Natalie is..." Helen let it hover in the air for a moment. "She's got to be in the middle of stuff, even if it's got nothing to do with her. Especially if it doesn't. And she's not good at asking 'bout stuff, either."

"Understood." Yeah, this wasn't going to be a fun day...

The other girls trickled in, one by one: Cynthia with a bright red ribbon on her ponytail to match the poodle skirt she was wearing; Katelyn with her bangs brushed back for a change, revealing hazel eyes; Shelby in denim overalls, curly hair held by a green band; and Claire, also in denim overalls but also sporting a t-shirt with the happy yellow visage of an electric rodent from the world's most popular monster-catching game. The little anime fan had a headband with pointy yellow ears to match it.

"Gotta be the best fan, huh?" Uncle asked her.

"Like no one ever was!" came the enthusiastic reply.

"Okay, then!" he said as the giggles died

down. "I got a text from Natalie's dad saying she'll be a little late, so let's go over our characters first. Now, there've been a lot of emails flying around this week.." And wow, was that ever an understatement. "...and a lot of little details worked in. Some of these everyone knows. Other stuff only your individual princesses know for now. And of course," he said with a malicious chuckle, "there's stuff you won't ever know until it's too late. But for now, let's keep to the present. The princesses have arrived in Pazh Milna, capital of Carpazha, after a few more days on the road. They've had some time to rest and recuperate. So what've they been up to?"

"We're writing letters to home!" Claire shouted ahead of the rush.

Uncle didn't even bat an eye at that one. The little anime fan had come up with much weirder ideas in previous game sessions, so this seemed pretty normal in comparison. He even had a few ideas of his own, gleaned from an internet forum years ago, that would fit here.

It was a quiet afternoon in the Laughing Cat

Inn, the third which the gathered princesses had enjoyed so far. The little establishment on the outskirts of Pazh Milna was a cozy structure of chalk blocks, dark grey mortar, and orange-red roofing tiles that was snuggled in between a gaggle of identically constructed neighbors. From the second-floor patio, one had a wondrous view of the deep blue Sea of Peace, and the rates were quite reasonable, even before they had bargained with the owner to pay in fruit off of Flora's Staff of Plenty.

In the past three days, the staff had produced diminutive, thimble-sized oranges, crisp pears with sandpapery outer skins, and a pair of huge, spiky fruit like nothing anyone had ever seen. The first giant of vegetation had weighed in at almost twenty pounds all by itself, tasting sweetly sour when raw, but its smaller, unripened brother had tasted more like pork when roasted. The innkeeper saved all the seeds from everything, treating them like gold in hand. All in all, it had been a good, if spontaneous, choice on Bianca's part. When the little witch had seen the inn's placard with its smiling black feline, she'd immediately insisted on staying there.

Right now, each of them was concentrating on writing. There was a message service just around the corner that helpfully offered sheets of creamy white paper, small bottles of ink, and cheap quills for mere pennies, and Princess Cassandrella had finally nagged the others into agreeing to let their families know how things were going.

Princess Gwenevrael, daughter of King Artundus of the Fifth Court and duchess of the Lonely Grove, wrote with a flowing and graceful hand that would have met with the approval of her childhood tutors. Her words were just as courtly, couched in vagaries and nuance as she tried to relate the events of the last week in a way which would not scandalize the court. Gwen was quite deliberate in the way she referred to her new friend, Selvi, and no one reading the missive would realize the barbarian princess's origins.

Selvi Khan's-daughter, on the other hand, had very little use for the written word. She was literate, despite much argument with her mother years ago, and it was only after seeing her father going over reports from the hinterlands that she came to realize its use. Her letter now resembled one of those reports, crossed with a bit of warrior's epic. She went into great detail on the specifics of each battle, but skipped some details concerning her new friend, Gwen.

The letter of Princess Flora Fidella Del'Monica was more lyrics than prose, as she strived to pen verses worthy of their adventures so far. She had spent much of the last three days studying with the bard who called the Laughing Cat her second home. Her time with the woman had helped provide context for many things her Uncle Alviss taught her over the years, including her favorite methods for communing with nature. It would take a lot of practice, but she figgered she could find a way to bring together bard-craft and her druidic heritage eventually. Along the edge of the paper, she scratched in a long series of lines – some long, some short, some slanted this way or that. It looked like some a random scribble, unless one was in the know about the secret language of the druids and its written form.

The piece of paper on the table in front of Princess Cassandrella was remarkably pristine, with only a small portion of its surface filled with carefully drawn but slightly blocky letters. The moon princess had taken far longer to start than the rest, not wishing to spoil the creamy lunar pallor of the page with unnecessary scratchings. It had also taken her some time to find a way to describe the past week in a way that would place her blessed mother the high priestess of Selunika into a state of apoplectic conniption. In the end she'd elided over the encounter with the thieving ant-folk ("a wonderful picnic, but for the pests"), downplayed her run-in with the malevolent mushroom men ("time spent meeting the common folk of the forest"), and outright fibbed about the fight with the murderous rosebush princess ("an afternoon's entertainment with a lady in her garden; her voice must simply be heard to be believed"). Prevarication and equivocation were big, scary words to her, so she tried not to think of the letter in that way. It was... an exercise in creative writing; that was all. To soften the blow to her conscience, she doodled in the picture of a happy bunny rabbit next to her signature.

If ink were blood, then Princess Bianca had absolutely murdered her letter home. There were furious scribbles, cross-outs, and lines that veered off to form separate thoughts so that the finished missive looked like some sort of literary hydra, dripping blackish ichor all over the castle rugs. Her words held some clue as to why, though it would take much analysis before anyone could decipher the handwriting. The little witch was bristling with anger at Gran'Mama, with each spiky loop and bloody tittle like a stab at the old bat's face. In the past few days, she'd finally broken down and had a professional take a look at the fancy magic rod which she'd been gifted with, and as she'd suspected, the thing was nothing but trouble – a wondrous rod that randomly supplied one of twenty or more random outcomes, like some uncaring deity were rolling dice every single time she activated it. Not all of these outcomes were advantageous for her. Case in point: the other reason that her letter was such a mess was because Bianca was hardly larger than her own feline familiar, and it was all because of the rod's capricious nature. She needed both hands to properly write with a quill.

"Okay, that's all for me," Bianca said as she signed her name. She dotted the i with all the force she could muster, blunting the quill and spattering ink.

She rode her broom down to the ground floor, while the others took the stairs. It was a little lazy of her, yes, and it certainly attracted the stares and mutters of the locals, but she wasn't about to struggle up and down those steps if she didn't have to! The rest of the princesses were fast enough on their feet and caught up well before she reached their destination.

The messaging office was a funny little shop, hardly more than a shed built on the corner of a busy intersection. The lines were always long, but they moved quickly, passing beneath the sign with its green top hat fast enough to set it to swinging. Lined up along the back of the shed was a shelf full of hats jut like the one on the sign. To her witchy senses, each one tingled with power. Somewhere out in the wide world, Bianca knew, there were masters of conjuration, abjuration, and millinery who held the secret of making such hats and tying them into a grand network. Every court on the two northern continents, and perhaps those of the south as well, had similar enchanted headwear, capable of sending letters and occasionally small objects. For those who inherited the things, it was quite lucrative, and the local hatsman was more than happy to accept their shiny new Carpazhan shillings before sending their letters into the ether with a wave of his magic wand.

"Well, that's done," she groused as they wandered towards the nearest market plaza. "So, we did what Cassie wanted. Can we talk about where we're going next? Because I really —" She never got to finish that sentence.

"Hi, everyone!" Natalie Perkins flounced into the pizza parlor ten minutes late and seventy decibels loud. It wasn't just her voice; her shoes had thick heels that went *stamp* on the floor and her frilly top had bells that went *jingle* with her every step. There was no way humanly possible to ignore the ruckus, though Shelby and Cynthia tried.

"Hello, Natalie," Uncle said equitably, in the

misplaced hope that the girls would follow his example. "We were afraid you weren't coming."

"No, no, it just took longer than I thought to print off my character sheet." A sheaf of paper was thrust at him so forcefully that he almost lost the tip off his nose. "Here she is, Princess Isabel Cœur de Lion Solaire!"

"Princess?" Shelby had a sour look on her face.

"My suggestion," said Uncle. "We've got a theme going on, after all. But..." He thumbed through the pages. "This is a lot more than we discussed via email."

"Oh, Kyle had some last-minute ideas."

Uncle was pinching the bridge of his nose as he skimmed through. "So I can see... Okay, I can let you get away with the celestial heritage, since it fits pretty well with what we discussed before about the solar paladin bond, and it gives your character a few more options at the lower levels. The Headband of Precocity goes well with it, too. But I'm going to have to nix the flying unicorn mount, the bridle of invisibility, the lasso of truth, and... I'm kind of tempted to let you keep the Holy Hand Grenade of Antioch, just with a geas that makes it impossible for you to count to three properly... but nope," he decided with the scratch of a red pen. "Most of this stuff is well beyond what a level five paladin should have."

Natalie jingled as she rolled her shoulders in a shrug. "Eh... Kyle said you might say that, but it was worth a shot. So, what's going on?" She dragged a chair over to sit beside Claire and produced a dice bag from her little purse. "We started yet?"

"Just getting to it," said Uncle. "While I get your spell cards organized, why don't you introduce us to Princess Isabel?"

"Hello!" a voice interrupted the princesses' conversation, stopping Bianca in mid-sentence. The owner of that vigorous contralto swept through the market crowds, parting them like some prophet of old. Heads turned and eyes stared in eye at the sight of the paladin as she made her grand entrance. The young woman was tall, almost of a height with Selvi, and clad in a lithe, flexible armor whose enchantments had obviously cost more than its burnished, golden metal. Her head was bare, black tresses falling perfectly out from under a golden headband fitted with a diamond-shaped stone, like a third eye in her forehead. Upon her chest was a blazon, the sun in all its grandeur with rays of red, white, and blue radiating from it.

The princesses stared along with everyone else, unsure of what they were seeing – except for Cassandrella, who cautiously asked: "Izzy? Is that you?"

"It certainly is, Cassie!" The paladin beamed.

"Um, ladies?" the moon princess said, all too aware that four pairs of eyes had transferred their stare to her. "Let me introduce to you my cousin. Princess Isabel Cœur de Lion Solaire, granddaughter of the High Priest of Solastria."

"Wait, wait," Shelby interrupted. "You two are sharing a backstory now?" The black-haired girl's suspicious stare was enough to wilt Claire at twenty paces, so across the table the girl was practically melting into the checked tablecloth.

"I'll take credit for this one," Uncle said quickly. "Natalie's princess needed a good reason to be introduced into the party, and I didn't want to wave my hands and go 'Poof! there's a paladin!' or something equally ridiculous. It makes sense that a moon princess and a solar paladin might know each other, so I went with that. Got a problem with it?" he asked, metaphorically spearing the little naysayer with an arched eyebrow.

"Nah, guess it's okay..." Shelby's face, all scrunched up and fuming, did not match her words one bit.

"Okay, so before we get started for real," Uncle continued, "We have some things to go over. First, Natalie. Your brother said he'd give you the basic run-down on how things work, and I'll be happy to fill in the blanks as we go. Any burning questions right now?"

"Nope!" the girl shouted, raising her dice bag and shaking it loudly. The bells in her sleeve were louder still. "He even let me use some of his extra dice!"

"Good. Now, something new for today..." He drew a small stack of laminated rectangles out of his bag and removed the tangle of rubber bands holding it together. Each one was about the size of a trump card, cut from bright red construction paper and featuring a crest, a pizza with crossed swords, glued to them before lamination.

"These represent Hero Points. Whenever you need a second chance on a bad roll, or want to improve your chances of getting some incredibly brave and reckless action to work, you can play the hero card. The full scope of their usefulness is up for discussion, but if I say no, then that means no." He passed one card to Natalie and two to everyone else. "Generally you get one card just for being an adventurer, and another anytime I feel like you earned it. After last week, you all definitely did."

"So what do we do now?" asked Shelby.

"I should be asking you ladies that." Uncle lay out a sketchy, hand-drawn map. "Here's the basic outline of the area you're in, known to elven scholars and cartographers as the Hundred Kingdoms, because they can never bother to count how many actual countries are currently within its borders. Knowledge checks, ladies."

Five large dice clattered across the map, followed belatedly by Natalie's metallic twenty-sider. Three of them came up 18, 19, and 20, lined up neat like peas in a pod.

"Not bad..." Uncle said as he passed sticky notes to Claire, Natalie, and Shelby. "Now, let's put that knowledge to good use."

The Laughing Cat's main room was largely empty in the mid-afternoon, and the five – now six – princesses had a table to themselves. It was big and ancient as pieces of furniture went, and carved from a single massive tree trunk. At the moment it had a map unfurled across its face.

Gwen was proud of that map. While not of elven make, it did not offend her sensibilities when she looked at it. Now she could only wish to understand it properly. The region of the Hundred Kingdoms was considered a constant source of headache for elven cartographers, who preferred their political boundaries to remain constant for at least a century at a time. The human lands which lay between the Sea of Peace and the Broken Sea further west were a patchwork of shifting alliances, fealties, and languages. Even with the gossip of classmates, many of whom actually lived in this stretch of the continent, the half-elf's knowledge was sorely out of date.

"What are these?" she asked, tracing a finger along a series of thin, spidery letters. Many of the northern cities on the map had names written in both that script and the blocky letters of the common alphabet.

"Palachkit cursive," answered Selvi. The half-orc grinned toothily but otherwise did not call her out for her ignorance. "It's still used in parts of the khanate, though most Palachkit-folk moved south in my great-grandfather's time."

"And conquered all the poor people of the northern kingdoms." Isabel sniffed. "It's been a terrible time in some cities, suffering under Palachkit overlords."

The khan's daughter shrugged. "No skin off my nose. It's not like they killed all the locals when they moved in or nothing."

"There were wars," countered Isabel. "People died."

"And there'll be wars again," said Selvi. "Fightin's about the only thing that's constant around here. Someone's always fightin' something, and often for stupid reasons."

"Your people drove the Palachkit south and west! Don't you feel the least bit responsible?"

Another shrug rolled off those armored shoulders. "From what I heard, the Palachkit moved on their own, 'cause they didn't want to live under anyone's law but their own. Goody on them.

We still gotta decide where we're gonna go, though."

Princess Bianca had one tiny hand up in the air and waving frantically. "Um... Is Ranshangban anywhere on this map?"

"Definitely not," said Gwen. She knew that much about western geography. "That's far to the south, past the desert lands, even."

"Past the desert, huh..." The little witch clambered up onto the table to get a better view. "Well, darnit. That's what I wanted to tell you all about earlier. I finally deciphered that note I grabbed back at school."

"The one you took from Mistress Penskill's personal folder?" Cassie asked. The moon princess still wasn't too happy to have been a part of that little incident. "I thought you said you couldn't read the second page?"

"What do you think I've been up to these past few days?" said the witch. "Well, aside from identifying magic items and researching ways to reverse a shrinking spell, I've been working through that stupid scrap of paper. It took a while to get through those old Pagosian runes the old bat prefers, and a while more to find a good Gnomon dictionary, but I finally figured out what it said. Or at least one part of it..." she mumbled off at the end. "Ahem, yeah. There was one paragraph that was really clear, and it was a question – to Lady Amberyll, I guess – suggesting that I should be allowed to visit my father to see if I could learn anything from his style of magic."

"Your father?" asked Flora.

"I didn't know wi... your people had fathers," said Cassie. "You all seem to be girls." The cleric blushed with embarrassment.

"Oh, we got fathers," said Bianca. "We just don't have much to do with them. Our moms pick guys with good magic backgrounds, have us, and then they're gone. So I don't know how Old Penskill knows something when I don't, and I don't know why she thinks visiting him is such a good idea, either. But I want to find out," she finished. Her mouth was twisted up into a good scowl, while behind her Jinkies had left off his mid-day grooming to give the other princesses a stare of his own.

"Ranshangban, huh?" Cassie considered. "Heard lots of stories about it. Supposed to be full of awesome magical stuff. That sounds like a cool place to visit!" The moon princess bounced in her seat and looked around excitedly. "Well? What do you all think?"

Gwen and Selvi shared a look. "Could be

fun..." the ranger began.

"... and it's about as far from school as we can get," finished the khan's daughter.

"I'm in," said Flora. "I mean, yeah, it's a long way, but we're on an adventure, right? We should see the sights and hear the music." She patted her lute thoughtfully.

"Okay!" Bianca squeaked. "It's settled! Now we just have to find a boat going south, and..."

"I must protest!" From her forgotten corner of the table, Isabel fumed.

"Oh, must you?" groaned Selvi.

"Yes! I came here to find my dear cousin and bring her to a place of safety, and I am not about to let her hare off into danger again!"

"It's okay, Izzy," Cassandrella attempted to soothe her cousin. "We've already had some adventures, and we all came out all right. Well, mostly," she added, looking at Bianca. "You don't have to..."

The paladin's fist rattled the tea saucers as Isabel slammed it against the tabletop. "No! I have a mission, Cassie! Prior Matthias received word of your plight, and ordered me personally to take you to safety!"

Gwen had her best diplomatic face on, the one she'd regularly used to deal with some of her more temperamental cousins at court. "Look," she began in a calm and low voice, "we've just met, and I know it may sound crazy, but we can take care of ourselves. We have so far, and that includes Cassie. In fact, I think she's done better than most of us."

"Helped me out in a pinch or three!" Selvi loudly proclaimed.

"Yeah, we need her, and she needs us!" Bianca squeaked. Her familiar mewed in agreement before returning to his bathing.

The paladin's face grew progressively more sour as around the table her cousin's merits were endorsed again and again. "Alright, alright," she grumbled. "You've made your point. Perhaps the reports were overstated..."

"And we would love to hear where you got them from," Gwen added. Cassie nodded in agreement. If her mother heard those same reports, coming after that letter home... The moon princess did not want to consider the consequences.

"But that does not," the paladin insisted as

she pressed on, "absolve me of my duties." Izzy's arms locked across her chest, and her mouth formed a most princess-like pout. Everyone else around the table could recognize it instinctively, and a collective groan was felt more than heard.

"Seriously," Shelby was saying. "What's your malfunction here? We're trying to get going, and you stall things over and over."

"You may be going, but it's the wrong way!" whined Natalie. The new girl had a pout to match her princess's. "Isabel is stationed in Nordiv, which is... er..." She searched the map. "Here!" She tapped the spot with a finger. "And from there it's a quick boat ride across the sea to where Cassie and her are from. Er..."

"Selunika and Solastria," Uncle provided.

"Yeah, there! Isabel is a princess with a mission, so let's get that done and then do more fun stuff."

Shelby turned her glare towards Uncle. He was prepared this time, and didn't even flinch.

"Are we really supposed to go along with this?" the girl demanded.

"It's your choice, ladies. Really." Well, in truth it'd definitely be easier if they went with Isabel, and the character could integrate a bit better with the group, too. He had contingency plans set up, however, and there was a flowchart pinned to his screen with a fork right at the start.

"Awright, then. Let's have a vote!" Shelby declared, thumping the table with her palm. "All in favor of heading south to that magic city, raise your hand... Good," she said as she counted. "And opposed... just Natalie. Sorry, Nat. We're not riding your railroad."

Uncle spoke up before the new girl could explode in a fit. "Yanno, as I recall, the mission oath your brother and I agreed on was simply to protect Princess Cassandrella. There's a lot of ways to do that."

"Yeah, but..." But she'd already made up a narrative in her head, he could tell, and she didn't want to abandon it yet. Especially not for something that took the spotlight away from her in any way.

"So let's give this a try!" he announced with a clap. "Isabel has reluctantly agreed to accompany the rest of you south, after properly reporting to the Temple via magic hat. She, Selvi, and Gwen all have horses now, while Cassie rides behind someone and Flora travels as a deer half the time." That detail got him a gap-toothed smile from Cynthia. "Bianca, of course, gets to ride on her broom with Jinkies. You're all going down this road..." He traced his finger along the map, starting from the dot labeled 'Carpazha' and ending at one labeled 'Namilda'. East of the route was the coastline, and west of it was a huge, brownish zone labeled 'moorlands'.

The girls' eyes all followed his digit, with so much attention being spent that they didn't even notice his other hand move until the dice rattled behind his screen.

"What was that?" asked Helen.

"Just a little something called the random encounter table," Uncle said innocently. None of them bought his act. "Okay, um, you're about two days south of the city when you run into something." He rolled again, checked the number against his flowchart, and then handed a note to Cynthia. "If you'd do the honor of having Flora introduce this one?"

"Ahem..." The pony-tailed girl read the prompt twice, which was the bare minimum for understanding Uncle's messy scrawl, thought for a moment, then began. "So, Flora's scouting ahead a bit..."

Of the various powers made available to her by her druidic heritage, Flora enjoyed the wildness of transformation the most. There was something indescribable about leaving your human form behind, if only for a little while, and coursing through the forest as a wolf or a deer. Though she'd only come into it recently, as the power in her blood quickened and rose to the challenge of a life of adventure, she'd already come to love the hours spent scouting in the forest.

In the branches above her, Mr. Chitters rattled off a warning. Flora slid to a halt, her dainty hooves sending a few loose pebbles rattling as she arrived at a clear space. The forest came to an end right there, with a few dozen yards between the scraggiest brush oaks and the rippling of the river. It was the height of summer now, and the waters were low, but fast where they rushed between many boulders. Still, it would not be difficult to go from rock to rock and cross the way.

Mr. Chitters called out again. What was he

on about? she wondered. She stood stock-still, taking advantage of the wide angle of vision her deer eyes afforded her, while her fuzzy ears flicked back and forth. These enhanced senses had taken some time and practice to get used to, so differently did they operate from her own. Vision in particular was tricky, because deer simply did not move their eyes the way people did. At a glance, she could take in almost everything around her, but her depth perception was abysmal. Only in a narrow zone where her eyes overlapped could she actually tell distance in a way that made sense, so while her eyes said something was down there, it took a few vital seconds to understand what, not to mention how far away.

Grumbling in her head, she quickly shifted back to human form to better take advantage of binocular vision. That was when the vague forms among the rocks came into sharp focus. It was also when the trio of oversized lizard-things noticed her. Raising their heads from their basking positions, they expanded bright red neck frills and hissed. Overhead, there was a rumble as thick clouds suddenly rolled in.

Selvi pushed her horse into a gallop as screams rang through the trees. Damnit, what had the druid wandered into this time? Flora'd made a habit of dancing ahead of the traveling part in the form of a deer or wolf, but that was the princess's own voice yelling bloody murder right now, only to be drowned out by the crack of lightning. The barbarian eyed the clouds as they streamed unnaturally across the previously blue sky. Whatever Flora had stirred up, it meant business.

Well, so did Selvi. When her horse balked at the noise and light, she dismounted and ran as fast as she could through the undergrowth. Behind her sh could hear the graceful step of Gwen's feet on dry leaves, along with the heavy thump of Isabel's boots.

Then the forest gave way to grass and river pebbles, and they were all clattering noisy as an orcish victory parade. There were definitely better ways to make an entrance, she grumbled to herself as the source of the commotion turned their heads and stared unblinking at the new arrivals.

Lizards. Why'd it always have to be lizards,

as the old captain of her father's honor guard would say. To hear the veteran orc tell it, the greater half of all monsters roaming the khanate and the wilds of the far continent were reptilian. The things before her now were a perfect example: each as tall as a pony at the shoulder, almost four yards long from snout to tail-tip, scaled and frilled.

In the sudden cloudy gloom, the flaps of scaly skin around the lizards' necks glowed pale red, with brighter veins of yellow pulsing faster and faster. A faint crackling could be heard, to be answered by a rumbling up above. Selvi felt the ends of her hair begin to stand on end.

"I'm gonna cast a spell!" shouted Natalie. The girl was waving a red-marked magic card. "Resistance to elements! That works for electricity, right?"

"That it does," Uncle confirmed.

Cynthia had her hand up now as well, but her face wasn't nearly as exuberant. If anything, it looked like she'd just sucked an entire lemon-flavored black hole. "That's a level-2 spell, ain't it? Is she supposed to have one of those already?"

"Yeah," huffed Shelby. "Thought paladins

didn't get spells till later than some other types. So how's she got something like that? Er..." The girl slowed down as she noticed the amused look on Uncle's face.

"Been reading, have you?" he asked the two of them. "And here I thought you weren't so interested in the game details."

Shelby muttered something that he couldn't quite make out, but he answered anyway. "As it turns out, you're right. Isabel would not normally have that spell, except that she gets it as part of the celestial heritage package at level five, and even then she shouldn't have a spell slot for it yet. That is why she chose as her heirloom the Headband of Precocity, which gives her that spell slot at one use per day. Also, I am being very nice in letting her get it at all," he added as a reminder to the paladin's player.

"Now, any other questions before we continue?" An uneasy silence answered him. "Okay, so Isabel's casting a spell to resist electricity, Flora's already called up a patch of tanglegrass to hold off the thunder lizards, and...?"

"Gwen is going to stick to the trees and shoot lizards," said Helen. "If possible, she'll give cover fire to Selvi." Two heads of hair, one blonde and straight, the other black and curly, huddled together to hash out tactics.

Katelyn and Claire were whispering as well. "Um, Cassie will ride around with Bianca on her broom and hold her action until someone's hurt." Beside Claire, Katelyn nodded and tapped a bomb marker.

"Looks like we're all set, then. Time to roll 'em, ladies..."

As she ran straight at the vile lizards, their harsh hiss rasping through her ears, Isabel knew only excitement. The Great Evil was a frequent fixture of temple lore, a scaled monstrosity which only birthed more monstrosity, and all her life she'd admired the icons of saintly warriors poised to strike down serpents, hulks, and even mighty drakes. One day, she knew, her name and face would be added to their number. Now seemed as good a time as any to begin the legend.

Which did not mean she would be completely reckless. Isabel knew something of the beasts infesting the edges of civilized lands, and recognized these from the tales of veteran warriors. While her right hand drew her shining blade, her left was pressed to her forehead, to the stone in her headband. Quickly she intoned a short prayer to the sun: "O Lustrous Light Above! Grant me the strength to withstand the power of these foul beasts!"

There was a faint crackling, followed by a tingling sensation which washed across her hand and on through the rest of her body. With a shout of glee, she raised her sword to the heavens.

Unfortunately, that was when the heavens opened up to send their reply.

Something, some primal orcish instinct told Selvi to hang back once the paladin began her charge. Let the new girl be flashy and loud; it would only serve to take the attention off of the rest of them.

But then things got very flashy, and much louder.

With a roaring crash, a line of searing yellow snaked down from the heavens, led on by the flowing lights of the lizards' frills. It didn't hit

Isabel, more was the pity, but it didn't need to. The rumble of thunder was enough to bowl the barbarian and the paladin over, with Flora barely keeping herself upright. The scaly trio were up on their hind legs now, frills flared open and snouts raised to the sky. When the lightning passed over them, the red veins in their frills glowed brighter.

An arrow whistled overhead, a blur that flashed through the air almost as quickly as the lightning had. One lizard hissed and clicked as the shaft suddenly sprouted from its head. A short second later, there was a small -boom- as one of Bianca's miniature explosives joined the half-elf's arrow.

Selvi struggled to stand, the urge to get into the fray and bust some scaly butts lending strength to her limbs, helped along by a desire not to look bad in front of the snotty paladin. It truly was a fight, in her head and limbs as much as on the field; there were still tingles pulsing all the way to her fingers and toes from the shock of even just a near-miss.

"Ha!" Not far ahead, Isabel was having no such problems, it seemed. The paladin danced around the injured lizard, hopping nimbly over its tail as it swung past, and delivered a coup de grace that about knocked its head clean off. "It's okay now!" she called out. "They need at least three together to call the thunder. Everything after this should be a cinch!" There was a self-satisfaction in he voice just asking to be punched, apparent even through the ringing of Selvi's ears.

A hand caressed Selvi's forehead, and the tingling sensation that swamped her every movement faded away. Her ears still buzzed a bit, so she didn't quite catch Princess Cassandrella's murmured incantations. It probably included the words 'Moon's Refreshing Light' or something similar. Though it hurt her pride, she accepted the moon princess's arm to help her stand up, and even muttered her own words of thanks. Cassie beamed like the moon at that.

She was helping! She was being useful! Princess Cassandrella felt like shouting to the moon, telling the whole world that she, the future high priestess of Selunika, was not just a burden on her friends. Lately it hadn't felt like that, despite all the kind words. Lately it had seemed like she was more in need of rescue than any fairy tale damsel one could name. That feeling of being ensorcelled in the witch's garden, her mind all stuffed with magical, musical fluff while her friends fought desperately on... That feeling she had not been able to leave behind when they'd quit the Lost Woods and its thorny memories. Having her cousin pop in the way she did, all ready to come to Cassie's rescue, had not helped either.

Isabel was facing off against another lizard now, this one much larger and more heavily armored than the first. Its frill flared wider than Cassandrella's outstretched arms, and its every move crackled with the snaps and sparks of barely contained lightning. Long rows of fangs seemed to glow from within the inner recesses of its mouth.

The breath caught in Cassie's throat as her cousin rushed at the beast, hacking at it with her broadsword. With loud clangs the blade bounced off, and with each loud failure Izzy redoubled her efforts to score a palpable hit on the thing, paying no heed to the popping sparks which filled the air. Not far off, Selvi was dealing with the miniature lightning in her own inimitable fashion. Roaring and raging, the barbarian princess simply ignored the sparks through sheer force of will. Cassie could almost see her eyes glow red to match the runes on her heirloom talisman, and spectral figures added their blades to her assault.

Seriously, how was a bunny supposed to compete with that? She settled back against a boulder and waited for someone else to need her healing services.

There was a sudden rumbling overhead, and Cassandrella looked up to see billowing purple clouds once more roll into position. But... how was that possible? Gwen and Bianca had done for the smallest of the thunder lizards, even before Izzy finished it off, and her cousin had said...

The boulder shifted against her back, rolling forward slightly before moving away. The moon princess fell backwards in surprise, and her ears were filled with a loud, heavy hiss. The next few minutes after that were harder to account for. They hurt, though.

"Look out!" Flora yelled the words, but Cassie never had a chance to hear. A thick, scaly tail smacked the moon princess as she tried to stand, and she crashed into the nearby rocks with a sharp crack. The lizard, so large that they'd first mistaken it for just another boulder, rose up on its pillared legs, flared its leathery frill, and brayed loudly with a voice that was part bird, part donkey, and all sorts of unpleasant.

Try as she might, the druid princess could

not find a place in her heart for this particular member of the animal kingdom. With another shout, she commanded her lute to take its other form, that of a massive, spiked club, and leapt to the moon princess's rescue. She could only trust that wood was not a good conductor of electricity, so that when she knocked a thunder beast upside the head — as she was doing now — she wasn't risking a massive electric shock in retaliation.

Sparks crackled and popped as the spikes bit into the beast's leathery hide, but her hands felt nothing but the shock of the sudden stop. Flora hopped back, jumping over the whipping tail like it was a game of skip-the-rope, then laid into the beast with all the strength her two arms could muster.

-whack- went the club, then -smack- on the return swing. A lucky strike landed right on its eye, and oh! how the beast roared at that! It reared up on its hind legs, opening its maw wide to cry to the heavens and call the thunder once more —

And that's when Bianca swooped in on her broom. A picayune bomb flew from a tiny hand, and it landed perfectly inside the thunder lizard's mouth, like the witch was herself playing some odd game with balls and baskets. However tough the beast's skin might be, in no way was it ever a good idea to swallow a live explosive. Unlike its mistress and itself, the bomb's boom was not small at all. The beast's remaining eye bulged, and smoke blew from its mouth and nostrils in the bare second it had before its entire head exploded.

A single, final bolt of lightning erupted from its body as it collapsed, rising upward towards the roiling clouds, and the clap of thunder almost rolled over the sound of a fifty-stone lizard falling to the earth. By the time Flora had recovered from the sound and the fury, Princess Isabel had reached her cousin's side. The paladin's glare was more baleful than any thunder lizard's.

"What were you thinking!?" Isabel shouted later that day, once they were safely bivouacked and had a few legs of lizard roasting over an open fire. The paladin, Bianca, and Flora had all taken turns patching up the battered moon princess, who despite it all still had to deal with a broken right arm and a couple of cracked ribs. There were limits even to magical healing, at least for the rest of the day. It wasn't as bad as it could have been – Cassie was left-handed, so she could at least handle herself – but it would still take several days' worth of healing magic before she could be said to be in adventuring shape.

Princess Isabel Cœur de Lion Solaire had doubts that her cousin would ever be adventure-ready, and was loud in expressing them. "Seriously!" she continued. "What were you thinking, rushing in like that?"

"Um... Selvi needed some help, and..."

"She's an orc! You can throw pretty much anything at them, and they'll be too stubborn to realize that they're hit! But you should know better, cousin."

"Hey, now!" Gwen interrupted. "There's no call for —"

"Oh, isn't there?" Isabel countered, swinging an accusatory finger at the ranger princess. "My temple received word that the heir to the Lunar Sepulcher had not only wandered away from a place of safety — a place that you cannot even show me on a map, I might add..."

"We showed you where it was," Flora noted. "Right there by the mark that said 'Here Be Dragons'."

"Whatever! Not only that, but she'd taken up dangerous activities with people unknown to the Temple, and presumably suspicious. Now, I was willing to give you all the benefit of the doubt, but..." She cast a skeptical eye around the camp. "But now she's injured, not a week out of the city gates, and it's all because of you!"

"I didn't see you defending her," Selvi countered. "As I recall, you were hacking lizards apart pretty enthusiastically a dozen yards away."

Isabel sniffed. "I was dealing with the most obvious threat," she said. "I trusted that the rest of you could pick up the slack, but apparently that was asking too much. Never fear, cousin dear!" she belled, holding Cassandrella close and ignoring the girl's winces of pain. "I shan't be so remiss in the future. Your safety is my first priority and mission, after all."

"You don't have to..." Cassie tried to say.

"But I must! You all should be thankful that I'm here to help you defend the next Light of Selunika. Such an honor is a weighty thing, even for the most righteous of paladins."

"And what are we, chopped liver?" Bianca muttered.

Isabel sniffed again, and her lip curled slightly. "No, I do believe that *you* are a witch, though your friends have been careful not to say. I shall not judge, or even call into question your claim of being a princess, for that is not my place, but please do not try to tempt us into strange midnight rituals without clothes on, or anything else of that sort."

"Actually," Bianca said with a grin. "That's more of Cassie's thing. Isn't that right?" She winked at the moon princess, whose face was now burning red beneath the heat of Isabel's solar glare.

"Um! It was only the one time!" spluttered Cassandrella. "My first full moon at the Academy, and I wanted to do something special, but it was so drafty without my small-clothes on and there were mosquitoes and sand burrs and I never tried it again so please don't tell anyone back at home please Izzy!"

"Well..." Even the paladin was taken aback at that verbal avalanche.

Gwen decided it was time to speak up. "Why don't we have dinner and get some sleep," she suggested. "In the morning we can finish tending Cassandrella's injuries and be on our way to Namilda."

"Yes..." Isabel's mouth had gone as straight and shut as a closed portcullis in front of the castle gates, but she was still nodding. "Yes, it has been a stressful day. I... need time to think. Do you mind if I take first watch?"

"Sure," said Gwen. Selvi just grunted while the others shrugged.

"I can keep you company for a while," Cassie said.

Her cousin smiled. "Yes, I'd like that."

Uncle breathed a sigh of relief and let the heady aroma of fresh-baked pizza fill his lungs. As usual, Max's timing was impeccable, as the pies could not have come at a better moment. That first encounter had taken far longer to complete than it should have, and only because the girls couldn't stop arguing. He sighed as he put the little figurines — mostly of Japanese cartoon monsters, repainted for variety — back in their box. The gaming session wasn't a total washout yet, but it was getting there. He'd played with groups that'd given a similar vibe as today, often right before they broke up for good.

Hope sprung eternal, though. The first two sessions had been excellent, far beyond anything he could've expected from a bunch of rookie players, and it was all due to their table dynamic. Surely one new kid couldn't ruin all that...

"Hey," Natalie whispered to him, passing a note. It was an unexpected piece of game etiquette, probably gotten from her brother. Break times were an excellent moment to send the game master a message and conspire without the others knowing exactly what was up. And who knew? Maybe she had a good idea that would help move the game's story along.

He read the note. He read it a second time, and then a third. Inside, he could feel his little wellspring of hope begin to dry up.

"She did *what*!?" Shelby shouted. Both her palms slammed down on the tabletop hard enough to make the pepperoni jump off her pizza. Any moment now, she'd be making angry duck noises out the sides of her mouth.

"You heard me," Uncle said with a sigh. In the past five minutes, he'd pulled Natalie and Claire aside for a quick chat and some dice rolls, and now the consequences were playing out. "Apparently Isabel and Claire had a long heart-to-heart during their watch, and when Selvi woke up to take over, the two of them were gone. Vanished. Vamoosed. Nowhere to be seen."

"Kidnapped." Now Shelby was drilling holes in Natalie's skull with her eyes, but only for want of power tools.

"You don't know that," said Uncle, "and in fact you can't and won't know anything for sure until you find them, because Natalie and Claire will be joining me at a table on the far side of the restaurant to play through their part of this debacle while the rest of you ladies chow down. Then, we switch. Got it?"

"Save some pie for me!" chirped Natalie.

"No promises," Shelby muttered.

The woods were dark at night. That really should've been a no-brainer, but Cassandrella hadn't considered it too much before. Most of the time, she had her moon-vision spell handy for situations like this, but that required planning and foresight and the wisdom not to go running off into the forest when one hadn't prepared the right spells that day. She caught small glimpses of the bright yellow moon through the branches overhead, but she couldn't find the serenity of mind she needed for prayer. Her arm and her ribs protested painfully with every bump, and no matter how carefully Isabel directed her horse, there were a lot of bumps.

There was a light in the paladin's eyes, a literal bit of sunshine from her blessed heritage that kept her sight clear and true, even in the darkest of hours. Cassie could trust in Isabel's eyes. It was everything else that made her unsure at the moment.

"Is this really such a good idea?" she asked, for perhaps the sixth or seventh time. "We could have waited till morning..."

"Sorry, Cassie," her cousin said, also for the sixth or seventh time. "The others would never have agreed to it. We need to get you somewhere safe, somewhere we can get you fixed up properly and away from any dangerous monsters, and they're all still fixated on getting to Namilda. Namilda!" She spat into the wind as it rushed past. "It's all pirates and doxies down that way. No place for a proper lady at all, so I'm sure they'll be all right. There's no temple down that way, either."

"So it's up to Nordiv?" she asked. Their flight had been so spontaneous that she'd not been able to pin Isabel down to any firm details while at camp. Everything had sounded so reasonable when the paladin had said it, or hadn't said it as the case may be.

"Maybe in time, but right now the closest temple is in Bargoczy, on the other side of the moorlands. We cut across just south of the old battlefields and get there by tomorrow evening, probably."

"Um, have you been this way before?" she asked, fearing the answer.

"I've committed all the maps in my home temple to memory. Leave it to me."

Natalie's dice weren't really metal, though they had a steely finish lacquered over the cores of mundane plastic. They rolled as well as any, as the girl showed just now. Her twenty-sided die clicked and clacked on the blue-checked cloth of their borrowed table, stopping at 5.

Yes, the dice rolled well, but Natalie hadn't. Uncle tried to keep his best poker face on, but he knew from long experience that poker was not his game. That was why he had a game master's screen to hide behind, so the girls wouldn't see his reactions so well. His list of potential encounters was still clipped at the top of the screen, and the number 5 item on that list was something he'd hoped to spring on the girls anyway, given the chance. After all the stuff that had gone on the previous weekend, plus all the emails that had flown around since, this particular encounter had gotten some fun tweaking. Having only two of them be there for it was going to make things tricky, but if ever there were a pair who could manage a diplomatic solution...

He nodded slightly. This would be a good test of character, seeing how the girls reacted here.

"Okay," he began in a serious voice. "As you ride across the moor, the gloom begins to gather around you like a shadowy fog, blocking out the light of the moon. Your horse comes to a sudden stop, rearing and stamping as a dark figure rises from the ground before you..."

There was a loud shriek from the horse as it flailed its front legs and shook the ground with its stamping. Cassandrella held on tight to her cousin with her good arm, and tried to make out just what was in the way. One moment, the flat span of heather and turf was clear and empty, a perfect route for the paladin's horse to follow, and then suddenly someone was there, standing like they were rooted in place.

That someone stood as high as the horse's shoulder, and was clad head to toe in ornate armor. Battered and dented, rusted and bloodied, the only part of it that could be described as in good condition was the blazon of a rose over the breastplate. A warrior's mask hid the face from view, and perhaps that was for the better. Its voice was a booming whisper, cold and lifeless except for the barest hint of anger.

"Who crosses my path on this dark night!" challenged the figure. "State your name!"

"I am Isabel Cœur de Lion Solaire!" Izzy replied. "Paladin of the Temple of Solastria, serving in the city of Nordiv. I ride in aid to my friend and cousin, who requires medical attention. Now let us pass."

"No..." A cold wind whipped across the heather, blowing leaves and sticks across the ground. "Those who would pass must stand and face me with honor, for lost honor binds me to this place."

Isabel had her horse mostly calmed at this point, though the mare still pawed at the ground nervously. From the saddle, she looked warily at the armored figure. "Is this going to take long?" she demanded. "Only, I'm on a mission and I cannot spare much time."

"It shall take however long it is meant to take," replied that sepulchral whisper.

"I see..." said Isabel. "No, I don't think I shall, then." She slapped her hand against the sunburst blazon of her armor, rattling off a quick prayer as she did. "O Powerful Sun! who brings strength and glory, lend me your arrow in this dark time!" There was a flash, almost blinding in the depths of night, and when her hand pulled away, there was a long bolt of searing yellow light grasped within it. With a final cry of "Sun's Burning Ray!" she threw it at the figure.

The beam of light smashed into the armored chest, and the figure crumpled to the ground. Isabel kicked her horse into action, and the beast was only too willing to oblige with a fierce gallop away.

"Trickery! Dishonorable treachery!" screamed the armored figure, its voice becoming high and shrill. All around the field, ghostly hands reached up to claw and clutch, but at best grabbed only air. At worst, they were pulped by the heavy hooves of the paladin's battle-trained mare. And then the angry shrieks faded away, lost in the gloom behind them.

"Okay..." said Uncle after the last dice rolls were made. "That wasn't how I expected things to turn out."

"It was even awesomer, right?" Natalie beamed. "Nothing's gonna stop Isabel in her mission."

"Maybe, maybe not," Uncle replied. "The others will be following, after all, and they're better over wild terrain than you are. But let's get some pizza while it's still there to be had."

Claire perked up, more than any time so far that afternoon. "Yay!" she cried. "Pizza!"

Pizza Time!

"So what are we in for?" Shelby grumbled, fixing her frizzy black curls back behind her hairband. A massive infusion of mozzarella and pepperoni had improved her mood a bit, though she still gave occasional side-eyed glares towards Natalie, who was now enjoying her pizza and a captive audience at the other table. Claire was putting up a brave front, but even her smile slipped when the other girl had returned from the drink bar with three huge glasses of assorted beverage. Uncle shared the sentiment. The last thing anyone wanted was a hyper-caffeinated Natalie on their hands.

"A long ride through dark winds," said Uncle after a moment's imagining. "And whatever Isabel managed to stir up along the way."

"Oh, goody." Arms were crossed and a

pout was fully loaded now.

Helen flashed her brightest smile and fluttered her eyelashes. "Oh, Uncle..." she chirped. "Can't you tell us more, pretty please? With sugar on top?"

"Not till you run into it, I can't," he said firmly. "Gotta play fair here, so no knowing beforehand. And if you overheard anything, ignore it." Now he chuckled at the four matching grimaces around the table. "Time to practice a useful life skill, ladies. Imagine a wall running right through your brain, with everything you know on the one side, and everything your princess knows on the other. Nothing can pass over that wall to where she is."

"But the wall's just imaginary," said Cynthia. The pony-tailed girl was smacking loudly on some gum as she talked. "What's to keep us from sneaking stuff over anyway?"

Uncle shrugged. "Basically, just the promise that you won't. Princess's honor."

Now he had four deadpan stares ringing the table. "No offense," Shelby said after a moment, "but that just sounds stupid."

"Welcome to adulthood, ladies. Now, moving on..." He had out a laminated map of what was currently being called the moorlands and was placing rocks and things on its grid of spaces. "Helen, Shelby, Cynthia, roll to see how well you can track our runaways."

Ruby, emerald, and goldenrod dice clattered across the table, coming up 13, 16, and 10, respectively. Uncle nodded as he mentally factored in the appropriate bonuses. With a dry erase marker he traced a section of a path. "Well, you know they went that-a-way," he said. "The game is a-foot!"

Gwen and Selvi's horses tore up the heather as they ran. Just ahead of them, Flora and Bianca flew on the magic broomstick. A tiny string of fairy lights dangled from the stick, providing enough light to see a ways ahead. The ranger and the khan's daughter could see in the dark, but that did not mean the rest of them could — and that included the horses.

The first sign of trouble was when the lights snuffed out. The four of them came to a halt as Bianca finagled the spell back into power, but nothing seemed to work. The witch was about to give up when the area filled with ethereal silver light.

"Ha!" she cried. "I told you I could... huh?" It dawned on her that the lights were not coming from where she'd been calling them. Instead, the princesses were in the center of a wide circle, ringed all around by tiny, wafting spheres of silvery flame. Just outside the circle, dark and broken shapes pulled themselves up out of the ground to form a second, more gruesome barrier.

"Oh, crap." Selvi and Gwen were already reaching for their swords.

"Stay your hands." The voice was echoing and cold. It was also right behind them.

"Wah!" Bianca almost fell off the broom just then, and Jinkies hissed in shock. A figure in twisted, broken armor stood on the moor like it had risen straight up from the ground. Perhaps it had. Its metal was battered and rusted except for the blazon of a rose upon its chest, and its face was completely enclosed in a masked helmet.

"Hear my challenge, mortals," intoned the figure. "And know that I am rather testy tonight. None shall pass here unchallenged, and no shenanigans this time. There's been enough of that already."

"Already?" Gwen's ears perked at that. "Has someone else been through here? Perhaps two young women on horseback?"

"That is not of importance now, though if you should best me, then perhaps I shall say something."

Selvi Khan's-daughter rolled her shoulders and grinned a tusky grin. "Best you, eh? So it's a fight you want."

"A challenge. A duel, fairly fought and witnessed, such as I never had in my life before," said the armor. "One of you shall suffice for all, but be warned; my cohort will deal with those who would interfere." Behind the circle of ghostly fire, the shapes solidified into skeletal soldiers, armed and armored.

"We can think our way out of this," Gwen whispered, but Selvi shook her head.

"This is a challenge, and a point of honor. Hai-ya!" she cried. "I am Selvi Khan's-daughter, of the Clan Dungivadim! I accept your challenge under the Rules of the Khans and the honor of my ancestors! May I have your name?"

"In time," came the answer. "If you have earned it."

"Well then," Selvi said as she drew her scimitar from its bindings. "Shall we get this show started?"

"Yes..." The armor reached down and pulled from the ground a pole with a ragged banner dangling from the end. "This is the standard of my troop. I bore it proudly, even to the day I died." Planting the banner firmly in the ground, the figure reached down again and drew a long blade, a knightly sword whose silvery perfection was completely at odds with the rusty metal gauntlets which now bore it. "And this is the blade Starsinger," the armor announced. "Forged by the dwarves of the far north for my ancestors centuries ago. Does your blade have a name?"

"...Wityula," Selvi said. "It means 'Whistler'. No one's ever asked before."

"Then let the singer salute the whistler, and the whistler return in kind, so that this duel may commence!"

Near the edge of the ghost-fire, Flora sat on the sidelines with the others, staring wide-eyed at the combatants as they circled. Duels were rare in her homeland of Silvalachia, and while her own father had turned out many a sword from his forge, they'd all been utilitarian things, good for the common soldier. These blades were different. They sang and shone in ways that could not be completely explained by the mundanities of wind and light. Though different in shape, both were slashing blades, and the two duelists were quick to step in and out of range to take advantage of an opening. There were no great clashes of blade on blade, and the strange, predatory dance looked nothing like any fight she'd ever seen in a stage play.

A dance... Her fingers itched, and of their own accord began strumming a tune to accompany the action. It was a wild thing, like nothing she'd ever played, and it swirled around the two like a mist. The strings screeched as Selvi slipped and took a hit to a padded shoulder, and sang loudly as the khan's daughter rallied with a terrible blow of her own. With fingers glued to the strings and eyes glued to the fight, she played notes to witness each swing and dodge, each hit and each miss. She hoped she remembered it all afterwards.

Selvi heard the music, though she hardly acknowledged it. Whoever her opponent was, he was a strong fighter and well trained. It had been ages since she'd last had a sparring partner of such caliber, and despite the circumstances, despite the pressure of time upon the moment, she was enjoying herself. The armored figure did not pull any blows, and her shoulder ached furiously from beneath its padding, but neither did she hold back.

The music surrounded her, speeding up as she rushed in, slowing as she pulled back, as much directing her movements as it reacted to them. Selvi could almost feel the fight's conclusion before it even came to be, before her opponent overextended on a swing and she ducked in to strike. A single, forceful blow to the sternum, and the suit of armor lay prone on the ground with its sword a yard distant.

She place her scimitar upon that armored neck. "Do you yield?"

"I wish," came the hollow rattle from deep with the metal. "But I cannot, for that is my curse. Honorable combat, but not honorable retreat. You shall have to slay me now, for I will not cease my attacks otherwise."

"No."

"What?" The question was echoed around the field of honor, from the living and the dead alike.

"You heard me. No, I will not kill you. Not like this, with your weapon gone and you lyin' there helpless," Selvi stated. "That ain't part of the Code or the Rules. If we'd entered this fight as sworn enemies, it'd be different, but this is a formal challenge, and killin' you this way ain't honorable." The khan's daughter withdrew her blade and stepped back. "So get up, and let's finish this the right way."

"Selvi, are you crazy?" Gwen called. "We don't have time!"

"Always time for honor, pointy-ears." Selvi nodded as the armored figure stood. "Whenever you're ready."

"In a moment..." The figure waved a gauntleted hand, and the skeletal warriors surrounding the field faded away into the shadows. "Whatever the outcome, I would act honorably by you, as you would by me. The young ladies you seek fled in that direction," it said, pointing. "Less than an hour ago, perhaps. They cannot have gone too far hence, even if they can avoid the other haunts which plague this bloodied battleground. You shall find them soon enough."

"Ah, thank you," said Gwen.

"It is the least I can do," said the figure. "And now, I should introduce myself properly..." Two heavy gauntlets took hold of the helmet, breaking through the layers of rusty metal with a dull crunch and pulling it away. A spectral head appeared, almost solid except for when it moved, and then the barest hint of a skull could be seen. At rest, the face was milky pale, with a dark spattering of freckles, a snubbed nose curving up to shining green eyes, and close-cropped hair the color of a bonfire.

"My name," said the specter as she picked up her sword, "which I now freely give to you all, is Rosina Garlinda Tatannus, third daughter of the Rose Throne of Baragoccia and unfortunate casualty of its final war."

"Any relation to Rosalind?" Bianca asked before anyone could think to put a hand over her mouth.

"Perhaps? I had an Aunt Rosalind, and a great-grandmother, and perhaps a niece or two by that name as well. Royal tradition," Rosina explained. Without the helmet, her voice sounded far closer to normal, though it still had a wavering echo to it. "Most women in my family had names that were a variation on rose. Why do you ask?"

"No reason!" Flora and Gwen shouted in unison, their fingers firmly engaged around the little witch's face.

Selvi rolled her shoulder some more to get the kinks out. There was certainly a masterful bruise already formed under the padding, and it was going to ache something awful in the morning. For the khan's daughter, that just meant she would have to get back to the action right now. "So, we gonna get started on round two?" she called to her opponent.

"Verily," replied Rosina as she brought her sword up for a salute. The scimitar sometimes known as Whistler rose up to return the gesture. Dark orcish eyes met ethereal green, and with a shared look the duel began anew.

Whistler had some advantages over Starsinger, Selvi knew. Just by looking at Rosina's sword, she could see that its longer range also meant that it had an area closer in, a strike zone where it couldn't possibly hit as hard. Selvi's scimitar, curved and angled the way it was, fared far better at that distance. It was simply a matter of getting in.

Rosina slashed wide and high, with enough power to take a head off if a princess were too careless. Selvi wasn't, and ducked in to exploit the opening. Her eyes were up front, however, and not on top of her head, else she'd have seen the blade arc up and around, only to return straight down and pommel first. The rounded end of the hilt was not sharpened or pointed at all, but it hit between the shoulder blades with enough force to send her to the ground.

A pair of dice should not have been able to hold the attention the way these did, but every eye around the table was locked upon them. The ghostly knight Rosina's clear twenty-sider had just rolled a 20, and by now everyone had enough game experience to know that big things happened with a natural 20. All that was left was for Uncle to confirm the critical hit and describe what happened to Selvi. At this point in the fight, it was likely to be painful, if not fatal.

Shelby wasn't about to let that happen to her princess. "Hold it!" she said, pulling out one of her laminated Hero Cards. She slapped it down on the table with the pizza-and-swords emblem face up. "Not sure what all I can do with this, but I bet it's worth a try."

"Gonna force a re-roll, huh?" Uncle nodded. "Good timing. Okay, we're going to see how this goes. Whatever comes up, we have to stick with, understood?" At the girl's nod, he picked up the clear die and sent it flying across the blue-checked table once more. It rolled and rattled and finally, with much bated breath from the girls around the table, settled on 10. "Alright," said Uncle as he checked the sticky note for the current tally of bonuses and penalties in play. "While a ten is usually considered just good enough, it's not enough to hit Selvi. However, since Rosina's committed to the attack, she's left herself open again. Shelby, roll to see what your princess makes of this opportunity."

Shelby grabbed her ruby twenty-sider and steeled herself, with her tongue stuck out the side of her mouth like a pitcher winding up for a knuckleball. The die flew from her fingertips, careening across the field map like a baleful comet. It smashed through defenses and toppled more than one game piece, finally ricocheting off a notebook and coming to a full stop against the unmovable objectivity of Uncle's game-master screen. The topmost face showed two small digits:

20.

"Yes!" The dark-haired girl punched the air triumphantly as the others cheered her on.

"A truly heroic upset, yes," Uncle agreed. "So here's how it plays out..."

Selvi rolled to the side instantly, more through luck and intuition than any plan, so the Starsinger missed her as it came down once again, this time pointy end first. There was a space on the blade, she could see in that moment, where the edges were not sharpened, and instead could be used as a second handhold. Rosina was doing just that, using the extra grip to drive the sword down ever harder.

The longsword's blade sank into the ground almost to the haft, so forceful was the thrust, and for a bare second Rosina could not pull it back out. Her spectral face flushed with effort more imagined than realistic, for there was no blood left in her head. When Selvi's whispering blade snaked out, hooking under the rose princess's head and removing it from her shoulders, there wasn't the slightest drop spilt.

Rosina's head flew up high into the air, only to land with a light thump a short ways away. Phantasmal tears streaked down the image of her face, and her mouth formed the words "Thank you" as her body faded into mist. A moment later, there was only an aged, broken skull lying on the field next to a rusted heap of metal that might once have been armor.

The sword Starsinger was still stuck in the ground. Selvi carefully pulled it free, inch by steely inch. With a blade in each hand, she stood over Rosina's armor and gave a roaring bellow, shouting out to the night that a proud warrior had passed on in the proper fashion – with honor in combat. Against her chest, her dragonbone talisman glowed briefly, its runes spelling out new combinations as each glimmered in turn.

Selvi was used to it acting up by now; she paid it hardly any mind. She retrieved Rosina's banner, turned to her friends, sitting where the ghost-fire had been, and nodded. It was time to get their little moon-bunny back.

Uncle nodded as he looked around the reassembled group of girls before him. The red-checked table felt a bit crowded at the moment, if only because of the egos, emotions, and dagger-like glares flying all about. For her part, Natalie was an immovable mass of self-confidence and blissful ignorance towards all the grumbling she'd caused. He'd made extra sure that she and Shelby remained as far apart across the table as possible, and even so he was concerned.

"Everyone full up on pizza and soda?" he asked.

"A to the OK there!" Natalie yelled happily. A short burp followed. Her three large cups were conspicuously empty, and the girl had a jittery smile plastered on her face.

"Let's just get this mess finished," grumbled Shelby.

"How're we gonna play this?" asked Cynthia. "Jump to the conclusion or somethin'?

"Or something," Uncle said. He pulled a stack of small index cards from his bag and laid them out in a long row. On the first card, he placed a black chess knight, and on the third he added a white knight. "Isabel and Cassandrella start a bit ahead of you. If they reach the end of this row, then they've made it to their safe zone. Some cards have an obstacle or lucky event written on the underside. We'll ignore the ones you're on now, and continue from there. Natalie, you're up first. Roll a d6, please."

"A what?"

He sighed. "A six-sided die," he reminded her.

"Oh yeah!" A little grey cube rattled around, finishing with six dots on top. "Awright!" she said as she moved the white knight forward. She flipped the card over and read: "Caught in nasty brambles. Skip a turn. Aw, nuts."

"You're still way ahead," Uncle said. "Team Chasers?"

Shelby scowled as she rolled, but her mood lightened a bit when her die also came up with six dots. The card's underside was blank, so she rolled again. Only one dot showed that time, and the scowl was back full-force.

"Another blank," Uncle confirmed as she turned over the card. "Okay, Natalie, you're up again."

This time, the paladin's team rolled a four, and their card was even better. "Woohoo!" Natalie crowed at the sight of the word 'shortcut' and moved her piece another space to a blank card.

The pursuers rolled a three, then groaned in unison as their next card was revealed: the picture of a group of armed skeletons, waving their swords in the air.

"Sorry, ladies," said Uncle. "Better finish them off fast. For every two full rounds this battle takes, that's another roll Natalie gets."

There was a dark and mean flame burning in Shelby's eyes. "Don't worry," she said. "This ain't gonna take long."

Gwen was hardly surprised at all when a squad of skeletal soldiers materialized along their path. The way the night had been going so far, it could almost have been expected. Her sword was out and ready but, as it turned out, unnecessary. Selvi roared through the mob, spurring on her horse as she held the Whistler in one hand and the Starsinger in the other. Not a single skull remained connected to its neck in the wake of her passage.

"You realize that was your last Hero Card for a while, right?" Uncle asked.

The curly-haired girl shrugged. "Things were meant to be used, right? And that was so worth it!"

"It was awesome!" shouted Helen. Around the table, everyone nodded in agreement, even Natalie.

"Well, as it turns out, you've only been delayed by one round. Natalie? Claire? You've got only seven spaces to go. Ready?"

"Yeah!" said Natalie. Claire just nodded hesitantly, and cringed a bit from the looks which the others sent her way. The metallic grey die rolled, coming up with a single dot on top. "Phooey!" Natalie concluded.

The obstacle card was flipped over, and everyone stared at it for a moment. The words BIG BATTLE! appeared in multiple colors of neon ink with gold highlights, surrounded by jagged lines, star-bursts, and crossed swords. The combination hurt the eyes just to look at it.

"Um, a friend drew these up for a game a

few years ago." Uncle found himself apologizing in spite of himself. "Her sense of style back then left something to be desired."

"I heard that!" Max's voice came from the direction of the salad bar. The pizza shop's owner was busy cleaning and wiping, but she spared a moment to wag a finger their way. "And I don't recall you guys complaining at the time."

"Eh, we were all in college," said Uncle, as if that were explanation enough. "None of us had much sense yet. Anyhoo..." he continued, flipping through his list of pre-planned encounters. "It looks like Isabel and Cassandrella are in for some more adventure after all..."

She hadn't yet dared to voice her feelings completely, but Princess Cassandrella was rightly fed up with this little adventure. Her late-night mental fog had burned away under the solar glare of Izzy's bad decisions, and as far as she was concerned the first and most important question was, how was she going to get out of this?

Well okay, the real first question was how to bring up the topic with her cousin in a way that the paladin would not yet again dismiss out of hand, like she had on the last few occasions. The second was how to deal with the broken arm and cracked ribs, all of which complained more loudly than she ever could. Not even the bright light of the full moon above could lift her spirits, because even on its lowest gait Izzy's mare was still a bumpy ride.

"There's a hospitality house not far ahead," Izzy reassured her, not for the first time. "It was marked on all the old maps." There was a quavering in the paladin's voice when she said it, though. "Not much longer, and we'll have you safe and sound."

Cassandrella was all set to say her important words, tell her cousin exactly what she thought, late though it was in coming. Her mouth was open to form the words, but a low-hanging branch of a passing tree interrupted. Isabel ducked her head to avoid it cleanly, and Cassie did so as well, only the length of gnarled wood suddenly reached down and plucked the moon princess off the back of the saddle.

"Izzy!" she screamed. Her cry ended in a pained squeak as finger-like branches closed around her and squeezed tight. Up, up, up into the air she went, swung around as wood creaked and groaned like a choir of tortured souls. Her eyes spun, her stomach lurched, and she wished now that the moonlight were not so bright and clear, because she was not alone, high in the tree. There was a metal cage braced against the trunk, and it was not empty. Withered hands still clutched at the bars, and a mouldering face was just barely visible as she was brought in close. Its lips were pulled back in an eternal grimace, and it had long since lost its nose and ears to the carrion birds, but its eyes burned with a life that had no place in the waking world.

Despite the pain and the vertigo, Cassandrella found the power within her to scream once more. She didn't stop for the longest time.

"Cassie!" Isabel cried as her cousin was snatched away into the night. She reined her mare around to face the tree, whose skeletal trunk and branches cut the moonlit horizon like a stab wound. Around its roots, the earth pulsed and trembled, and as she dismounted and charged in, she could see grasping hands and other assorted bits coming together to form gruesome, patchwork things.

The sight of it all was, if anything, too unnatural. Her eyes took it in, but her mind refused to see it all, and that above everything else helped her to stay calm. A stubborn part of her monkey brain was solidly convinced that nothing that strange could possibly be real, no matter how solid a -thunk- her sword made when she whacked. She could have been facing one of her temple's animated practice dummies, for all the lack of fear she felt in that moment. No, she thought as an excited smile played across her face, this was no danger at all, merely the chance to show the glory of the Sun.

Several yards above, her cousin gave another piercing shriek. First things first, Isabel decided.

"Sun's Burning Ray!" She hurled the words and the bolt of fiery light at the trunk of the tree, then cheered gleefully as it exploded against the bark in a cloud of sparks. The gnarled thing shivered from its roots to the highest branch, and then there was silence.

And then there was a high-pitched shriek as Cassandrella was dropped from twenty feet up in the air. Isabel managed to catch her successfully, with a groan from her cousin which suggested that perhaps the ground may have been the softer option. The paladin's legs tottered and trembled, but she managed to deposit the moon princess on the ground without planting her own armored bum in the heathered turf as well.

"O! warm and life-giving Sun," she quickly mumbled through the basic prayer. "Bestow your healing touch!" All the gentle heat of a sunny spring day seemed to gather beneath her fingertips, to flow into Cassandrella's damaged body and ease her pain. The cleric's breathing became less troubled, and her myriad scratches ceased bleeding.

With a nod, Princess Isabel Cœur de Lion Solaire turned back to the real, important business at hand: destroying as many undead as possible. She could hardly wait to report back to Prior Matthias about what tremendous blows she had dealt against the enemies of the Sun!

"You're going *back* into the melee?" Uncle managed to somehow be astounded and yet not surprised at all by this development. "Cassie's on the ground there in critical condition..." On the board, the moon princess's pearly-painted chess pawn was knocked over. Claire had rolled an amazingly bad series of numbers from her sapphire-colored dice, and her girl had already been in the red health-wise when he'd taken pity and fudged a roll from behind his screen to let her escape the grasp of the death tree. He'd even arranged the little tokens for the zombies in such a way as to provide a clear avenue of escape.

He probably shouldn't be so nice. In fact, he probably would not have been so nice if a similar situation had occurred in the very first game session. There were some players and some groups that thrived on imaginary bloodshed and total party kills, much as they complained, and he was certain by this point that these girls were not narrative masochists. They wanted fantasy and excitement, and probably would not mind a character death if it happened in a suitably awesome manner, like getting exploded by ninjas or something. But this... two girls half-surrounded by zombies, and one of them in the negative hit-point range; that was not the right way to go.

But he was darned like an old sock if he could think of a way to get them out of this situation without resorting to pure *deus ex game-master*, and that sort of save would be almost as unsatisfactory. "Just to confirm," he said, hoping that the girl took the hint and the second chance. "You're going to charge at the undead and try to hack 'em to bits?"

"Yeah!" came the enthusiastic shout. Natalie was bouncing up and down in her seat, in a way that wasn't just connected to the amount of caffeine she'd had so far that afternoon — at least, not directly connected. "Um, I'm gonna run to the little girls' room," she announced over the gurgling of her stomach. "Might take a few, so she'll just keep at it unless something gets too close to Cassie, 'kay?"

"Alright," he sighed.

Everyone watched her skip and slosh her way to the restrooms on the other side of the restaurant, then turned their attention back to the matter at hand. "We've got two rounds before we arrive," Helen said. "Think you can hold out till then?"

"Maybe?" replied Claire. "I'm not sure how much I can do, honestly."

Uncle made some quick rolls for Isabel, then rearranged game pieces appropriately. He'd taken the liberty of doing a wisdom check on the paladin, and as a result Isabel had yet to realize that the undead were drawing her farther around the other side of the little hill crowned by the dead tree. Her horse, he noted, had actually rolled higher on wisdom, and was now far, far away from the action.

"To answer your question," he said when he was done, "not much. The only reason Cassie's still alive and reasonably alert is because she's got a high constitution score and is a lot tougher than she looks, but even so... She'd probably take lethal damage from sneezing too hard, what with the state she's in. Your only real options are to lay there and wait, and maybe pray."

Dark brown eyes, magnified many times by Claire's thick glasses, crossed with concentration. "Well, she's a priestess, so maybe prayer's what we need. Didn't we agree that Cassie and her goddess were closer on a full moon night?"

"That we did." Of all the girls, Claire had sent him the most emails over the past week to discuss possible things to work into the story. Uncle wondered if the little animaniac were headed in the direction he thought she was.

"Okay!" Claire stood up on her seat and leaned across the table to look him in the face. "I'm tired of Cassie having to be saved all the time. I'm tired of her getting pulled along into stupid hijinks without being able to say no. She's the Princess of the Moon, goshdarnit, and it's about time she made use of that. So she'll be praying her fuzzy bunny slippers off while the full moon's still in the sky," she announced, slapping two Hero Cards down on the table by her fallen chess piece. "And she really, *really* means it."

"Can you even use two of those at a time?" Helen asked.

"Usually no," said Uncle, "except in an effort to cheat death, which I certainly think is the case here. Well," he added, returning Claire's challenging stare, "I'm all for moving our little timetable up an adventure or two, but you're gonna have to roll for it. Those Hero Cards add a big bonus for you, but it'll still be a hard one. Ready?"

Claire didn't even bother to dignify that with a response. Instead, she held her sapphire-colored die up, and, after everyone had had a chance to blow on it for good luck, she let it fall...

Princess Cassandrella had thought she'd known a good deal about fear. She'd been afraid when they'd all fought the bug warriors, though she'd overcome it then. Then again, in Princess Rosalind's garden of thorns, she'd been scared out of her bunny slippers, and had barely been any help at all. Just that day alone, she'd been scared of the thunder lizards, the ghostly suit of armor with its booming echo, and the thing in the tree. Those were easy sorts of fears to work with, but then there was the fear of being caught doing something naughty, the fear of speaking her mind to her cousin, the fear of not living up to the expectations of her temple...

Well, as she lay there on the cold ground, her body chilled and achy, all those fears didn't seem so bad, seemed instead to be minor little things to be overcome or laughed at. They all bled away, to be replaced by something much stronger and colder still.

She wasn't scared now; she was terrified. Even as the rest of her was paralyzed by fatigue and pain, her heart beat like a caged animal trying to burst free. Any moment now, she was sure, it would smash a hole through her ribs.

Somewhere off in the night, she could hear her cousin fighting, and elsewhere there was the groaning and shuffling feet of the restless dead. She wanted to shut her eyes tight and pretend it all away, but the Moon would not let her. Its pale, calm beauty lay low on the horizon, almost kissing the top of the moor, and it was straight in her line of sight now.

-Please- she prayed silently, not trusting in her own voice. -O Loving Moon, who watches over us all, help me. Save me.-

The Moon glowed back stoically. -Why should I?- the soft light seemed to say in its quiet glimmer. -My light falls on the just and the wicked, on the living and the dead.-

-I know- she thought.

-My light is equal and unbiased, but it is not fair- said the Moon. -Do you accept that?-

-Yes-

-That bad things may be done under My light?-

-Yes-

-That you may have to do those bad things one day?-

If she had the breath to spare in her lungs, it would have caught in her throat just then. Was this conversation really happening, or was it all a product of confusion and blood loss messing with her head? She could not tell. Perhaps she was past the point of caring. Instead, she just answered:

-Yes-

-That the way of the Moon is the way of change?-

-Yes-

-The way of order?-

-Yes-

-The way of life and of death? The way of violence and of peace?-

-Yes-

-And you shall serve willingly, with all your heart and soul, in all aspects and phases of the Moon's light?-

-*YES*- Never had a silent word been so emphatic.

-Then so be it-

The light of the setting Moon flared, brighter to her than the Sun in that instant, but cooler, softer, like the familiar embrace of silk sheets and coverlets on her bed back in Selunika. It wrapped around her, comforted and soothed her, and she willingly let herself dissolve into its presence.

There was a new figurine on the table now. Four sets of eyes stared at it, confused. A fifth set beamed happily from behind thick glasses. "Yes! Yes!" Claire crowed as Uncle unveiled the newcomer. "Now the butt-kicking may commence! Full Moon Mangle! Moonlit Mayhem! Lucha de la Luna!"

"...what is it?" Katelyn asked.

"And a 'Why?', too," said Cynthia. "Maybe a 'When?' to top it off. Like, when did this get decided?"

Uncle waved them down. "Everyone sent me all sorts of ideas for their princesses, remember? Well, Claire and I tossed some stuff around about how to power up a moon princess, and this was one. Now granted, neither of us expected to have the opportunity to fit it into the story quite so soon, but it's not like the rest of the session's gone as expected, either. Speaking of which..." There was the rattle of dice behind the game master's screen. "Isabel just failed her spot check. Like, utterly. So don't tell Natalie what's happened unless she asks in-character, okay?"

Now five sets of eyes all winked conspiratorially.

Selvi Khan's-daughter did not need any tracking skills for the last leg of their search. The raucous screams were clue enough. The flashes of light as Isabel tossed sunbeams like snowballs, those were hard to miss as well. Among the rolling hills of the wasteland, the old tree made a good landmark, and they'd already been heading in that direction when the sound and light show began, but now they spurred their mounts to their fastest gait. She could only hope they were not too late.

But, as it turned out, they were just in time for something. What it was, that was harder to say. Around the little hill with its dead, dry tree, a dozen or more misshapen forms lurched in the shadows. Far to the left, almost behind the hill entirely, there was the flash and bang she associated with Princess Isabel. A bit to the right, Cassie lay in a patch of bright moonlight – unnaturally bright, like the heavenly body had focused everything on that single spot. Her moonsilk and mythril gleamed brightly, and then suddenly there was a most un-moonlike flash that overwhelmed her night vision and left her dizzy for just a moment.

In the spot where Cassie had lain, there was... something else. Selvi's brain was at a loss to describe what she saw. It looked a bit like a rabbit, in the same way her father's prized dire wolves looked like cute, fluffy puppy dogs. Pure white fur bristled over muscular legs, and long ears swiveled to either side of a glimmering horn that bent back into a sharply curved half-circle. The beast was crouched low to the ground, but even under all that fluff it had to be at least as large as Selvi.

Nearby, a trio of misshapen, mismatched revenants finished pulling themselves from the ground and shambled towards the rabbit-thing. All three had at the most an ounce of brain matter between them, else they would never have dared. With a shrill scream, the oversized rabbit bowled over the first, sending the rotting skull back underground with its forepaws. Then it kicked back, ripping the second undead in half. The third undead got to experience firsthand what it was like to be a carrot.

"By the blessed elders..." Selvi muttered under her breath as the brief spat of carnage came to a close.

"What is that thing?" Gwen had arrived just in time to see those teeth in action, and her face looked a pale green in the moonlight.

"Pretty sure that's our Cassie, though don't ask me how," the barbarian princess replied. "Hey! You two!" she hissed at Bianca and Flora. "Avoid the bunny for now, but see what you can do 'bout those dead bodies wanderin' round."

Flora hopped off the broom and pointed. "It's the tree; I can feel it," she said. "Everything that's wrong in this area of the moor is centered on it. If you can keep those shambling things off of us, we might be able to do something about it."

The barbarian and the ranger grinned at each other in the moonlight. "You heard her," said Gwen. "Time to whack some weeds while they make firewood."

"Heya, gals!" Natalie announced her return loudly, plopping down beside her cousin. "What's new... wow..." she said as she surveyed the battle map. "That's a lot of zombies. And everyone's all here now?" She pouted. "Darnit, I was hoping to get to the safe house, fair and square."

"Your princess has been busy," Uncle noted, tapping the girl's chess piece. "Five zombies and counting."

"Aw yeah!" Natalie punched the air. "Beat that, slowpokes!"

"It ain't a game," said Cynthia with a scowl. "At least, not like that it ain't. We're all in this together."

"That doesn't mean we can't keep score! Ooh..." Natalie had just spotted the amateurishly painted vorpal rabbit figurine in the thick of a zombie mob. "Boss monster!"

Helen was about to correct her, but Uncle shook his head slightly. "It's your turn up next," he told Natalie. "What are you going to do? You don't know anything about this new thing or what it can do. Too busy whacking zombies on the other side of the hill," he explained.

"I'm gonna run up and smite it!"

He was unfortunately not surprised, though he felt like pinching the bridge of his nose in exasperation. "Anything else? Possibly before the smiting?"

"Nah. What's there to know? It's a big monster with lots of other monsters around it, and it's not obviously breathing fire or anything, so I should be okay."

He could almost see the dice rolling inside

her head to decide how she'd react, with a penalty to her wisdom score lying on top of a natural 1. Total comprehension failure. Uncle had never seen such a bungled roll in real life, ever, but now he had to deal with it. There was a sort of sigh that only a truly exasperated game master could make, and even if he'd never made it before during one of their sessions, most of the girls recognized it for what it was. Natalie did not. "Well, then," he said. "Guess it's time to roll."

Quiet as he could, he rolled his own dice while Natalie's rattled across the table. How bad this would turn out, he left to the little twenty-sider. A 2... then a 3... He felt his shoulders relax a bit, even as Natalie crowed at her own rolls. It was silly, he knew, but also nice to have the hand of fate enforce karma on its own.

'Every day, in every way, I get better and better.' That was Isabel's personal motto, and she could almost feel it in action that night. As she waded through the undead mob, each swipe of her sword seemed to destroy two of them, and each bright beam of sunlight speared three. She didn't really have the time to note what state the undead were in to begin with, or she'd realize that they were plenty ragged already, but she might not have cared, either. What was important was the act of destroying their evil.

And then there was this new beast, risen up to challenge the Champion of the Sun. What hole it had come from, she could not say, but it was going to be running a long way from here when she was done with it. Somewhere in the back of her head, she idly wondered where Cassie had got off to, but she had a sort of sixth sense which told her that her cousin was all right. Those other questionable princesses had most likely pulled her away from the action. Oh well, she could always retrieve the moon princess from them again later. Once she'd finished with this threat, they'd all see how awesome she was, and that she was the obvious choice to keep her cousin safe.

So she batted aside the groaning undead like they were stuffed dummies, her radiant aura forcing them to the side as she passed. The beast was before her now, its hackles raised and its long teeth bared. Even it must sense the strength to be found in Princess Isabel Cœur de Lion Solaire, Paladin of the Dawn Order in the Holy Temple of Solastria, for it backed down with its ears pinned back in apparent confusion.

Isabel raised her sword high, calling to it all

the power of the Sun invested within her. Light like liquid sunbeams flowed across her, climbing up the length of steel, encasing it, doubling its size with a broad blade of sunshine laid over it. She would not even need to hit it directly with the steel, she knew; the light itself would be enough to damage and daze the beast, leaving it vulnerable to more attacks.

The blade of steel and sun streaked through the night, its ethereal fire coming down squarely on the head of the beast. Any undead would have been cleft asunder, rendered instantly into dust, but all there was to show for her attack was a faint *clang*.

The beast had caught the blade on its own horn, deflecting it away from danger. All the bright sunshine that had traveled with that blow dissipated, blown away like so much powder in the wind, and Isabel was left in the dark with only a slightly bent piece of metal in her hands and a very large, angry rabbit before her.

It finally dawned on her that something was not right here.

Natalie was a little slower on the uptake

than her paladin, Uncle figured. He was beginning to feel a bit guilty about giving her all that metaphorical rope, now that she was in the process of hanging herself with it.

"Whaddaya mean, it didn't work?" she was yelling. "Paladins have the power to deliver holy smitings, so that monster should be smote! Er, smited? Smitten? Something shoulda happened!" she concluded with a pout.

"What *should* happen is different from what *did* happen," Uncle noted. "Both actually and grammatically. Alas, as it says right there on your reference card, the ability's name is 'smite evil,' and the rule's pretty firm on that. No evil, no smiting."

"Well, how was I to know it wasn't evil? It was a big, hairy monster in the middle of a buncha zombies!"

He tapped another one of her cards. "Paladins have a spell called 'detect evil' for a reason, yanno. Helps to avoid situations like this. As it is, you wasted a smiting, got a non-evil creature really ticked-off, and now it's time to face the consequences."

"But, but..." Natalie's lip quivered. "I didn't know!"

"You had plenty of chances to find out," said Uncle.

"Nobody told me!"

"Ya didn't ask," said Cynthia. Beside her, Katelyn gave her emphatic, if silent, agreement with some vigorous nodding.

"Uncle did mention doing stuff before smiting," Helen pointed out.

"But you went and did it anyway," Shelby concluded with a grunt. "Seriously, it's like you didn't even really look at the board before deciding to kill the wabbit. You missed all sorta little details."

"No I didn't!"

Claire wiggled in her seat. Where she and her cousin had been sitting hip-to-hip for most of the afternoon, there was now several inches of space between them. "Where's Cassie?" she asked. "Can you tell me that?"

"Huh? Didn't the others evacuate her to safety?" Natalie asked.

"No," said Shelby. "And anyway, that was supposed to be your job, remember? We got here a little late for that."

The new girl wasn't looking nearly as ebullient now. "Um, she didn't get killed by zombies, did she?"

"No," said Uncle.

"Eaten by the ravenous beast?"

"Nope."

"Then what the heck's going on!?" the girl whined.

"Cassie is a moon princess," Claire tried to explain. "And... certain things can happen at certain times of the month..."

"Better just spill it, or she'll completely misunderstand again," said Shelby. "You're starting to sound like my mom when she had to make the talk to me about periods and stuff."

Claire took a deep breath. "Cassandrella prayed to the Moon for help so the Moon decided to change her into a giant bunny rabbit with a crescent horn in her forehead but it's only temporary and she'd never attack her friends!"

Natalie was staring at the board now, realization finally dawning on her face. "You mean that monster was..."

"Princess Cassandrella," Uncle confirmed.

"Whom you just attempted to smite with intent to kill, in violation of your sworn oath and in full view of her goddess in the sky."

The girl's response was short, rude, and –j while completely appropriate for the situation – was not something that should be on the lips of either a paladin or a twelve-year-old girl. Uncle didn't begrudge her the expletive, though. To be honest, the situation probably deserved a lot more cussing than that.

Realization was slowly seeping into Isabel's conscious mind, and it was not a pleasant experience in the least. Her hands refused to let go of her sword, useless as it now was, but her eyes never left those of the beast before her. It... the giant rabbit... rabbits were always Cassie's favorite... but, no! It couldn't be... Cassie couldn't be...

It had Cassie's eyes, dark grey with a rim of silver that shimmered in the moonlight.

The sword fell from her fingers, and words fell from her lips – the sort of words that would scandalize her blessed mother to hear coming from her darling daughter. Isabel was still mumbling incoherent profanities as the rabbit pounced.

Flora was distracted from the matter of the dead tree by another hideous shriek. Unlike the previous few, this one had come from a human throat, and her eyes flew to its source. Isabel was down on the ground, her sword a short ways away, and the paladin was now pinned under a good twelve stone of bunny rabbit. The druid princess kept a wary eye on them, but whatever Cassie'd turned herself into, she didn't seem in much hurry to kill anything that wasn't dead already.

A bit above her, floating on the broomstick, Bianca was also staring. "Should we, yanno, help?" the little witch asked.

"I think Cassie's got things well in paw," said Flora.

"Not what I mea... eep!" Bianca banked to the left as a crooked branch swiped at her. With a loud crack, Flora's enchanted club fractured the aging wood, and the entire branch came tumbling down to her feet.

"Think that's the last of the low branches," Flora announced as her lute returned to its proper shape.

"Goody."

Flora was about to suggest going to calm Cassie down — if that was even possible — when that pure white fluff glowed brightly once more. With a prolonged scream that was almost a howl, the giant bunny raised eyes, ears, and horn to the Moon in salute. There was a soft glow, to be answered by a very bright flash from the paladin's armor. The brilliant gold began to run, dripping from the metal like watery paint, until everything was left a drab grey that could hardly be distinguished from the round, even with the light of Bianca's little lamps to help.

Before her eyes, the Moon finished its descent below the horizon, leaving the night even darker than before. The rabbit's pale glow lasted a few moments longer, fading as it shrank in on itself, and Cassie's human self collapsed over the still form of her cousin.

"Can you handle things here?" she asked Bianca quickly. Most of the druid's work had been to suss out weak points in the wood; the dead tree was far too gone for her powers of green to have any positive effect on it. The little witch was going to have all the fun in a moment.

Bianca nodded. "Be careful."

That was easier said than done. Gwen and Selvi had done an excellent job of mowing down what shambling undead were left, but the ground was uneven and treacherous in the dark. The black energies of death were strong here, eclipsing the senses she would usually rely upon, and she also had to keep watch up above. With its lower branches broken, the dead tree was limited in its ability to grab things close-in, but its upper branches could bend farther out, and across most of the space between her and Cassie there was plenty of opportunity for a snatch.

-Jump!- her senses told her. Blunted as they were, she barely avoided the spear-like thrust of an old branch. The gnarled wood plowed into the lifeless dirt, sending up a spray of grit. Flora rolled to the side, feeling more than seeing a second branch crash down. With her war cry of "El Kabong!" her lute resumed its duties as a professional blunt instrument, and she shattered both errant tree trunks with quick smacks of the spiked club.

"Toad in the hole!" came the cry from Bianca, punctuated by a series of explosions. They went -bim-bam-bom-bam-BOOM! in neat order, hitting each weak spot on the tree just as Flora had directed. With a loud crash in the dark, the dead tree toppled over, falling to the ground in the exact opposite direction from where Cassie and Isabel now lay.

Flora smiled to herself. Despite what some believed, druids were not completely against violence towards nature. Every garden could use a bit of pruning, now and then.

Isabel was out cold when Flora reached them, and Cassie wasn't doing much better. The moon princess was shivering with exhaustion, and could hardly stutter out a few words of thanks before passing out in the druid's arms. Flora did her best to check her friend for serious injury, only to find none. Even the cracked ribs and broken arm had healed up, good as new, and she figgered that after a bit of rest, Cassie'd be fit as a fiddle.

The paladin, on the other hand... Flora wasn't sure what to do there. Isabel didn't seem to be hurt, aside from the sort of minor scratches one might get while thrashing barely animate undead. Flora took a moment to pray away the specter of disease, but otherwise there wasn't anything to do. Isabel appeared to be in perfect condition, except that she wouldn't wake up, no matter how hard the druid slapped her face.

After she realized that, Flora slapped it a few more times, just for good measure.

"But... but..." Natalie's lower lip had yet to stop quivering. The tip of her nose had already turned red, and now her eyes were puffing up. She looked about as shocked as her paladin must have been, with the only difference being that the girl was still conscious. Uncle figured this counted as a TKO, at least. Certainly, it looked like Natalie would totally keel over at the slightest push.

"But it's not fair!" The words ended with a squeak and a sob.

Uncle sighed. "We've been over this..." Repeatedly, but the girl needed everything spelled out at the moment. "Paladins are held to a higher code. There are consequences to breaking that code. Princess Isabel broke it in a spectacularly bad manner. So right now, she is stripped of all her paladin abilities, including stuff like her bloodline powers and holy armor enchantment, until she's had the chance to go through an atonement ceremony. Which will have to be done at a temple, and probably only after proving herself penitent, so definitely not today. We're running short on time."

And patience, he did not add.

There was silence around the table for about three beats and then, with a sobbing wail, Natalie was out of her chair. She streaked across the restaurant floor and into the girls' restroom. The door slammed behind her.

Max had been waiting in the wings, but now she swooped in to gather up dirty dishes. "Yanno," she said over the clinks and rattles, "I ought to spruce up the old powder room a bit, if you're going to be sending kids to hide in there on a weekly basis."

"It's not like I'm trying to..." Uncle protested.

"Ooh! Ooh!" said Claire. "Could you add a bookshelf with some comic books or something?"

"I'll keep that in mind," Max promised with a wink. "Anything else I can get you all?"

"Some aspirin, some antacid, and some whiskey to wash it down," Uncle replied, only half in jest. "You girls stay put. I've got to call Natalie's dad now."

"...and that's what happened, sir," Uncle finished. It hadn't taken Mr. Perkins long to get there after the phone call had been made, but the explanation had been another matter entirely. Try as he might to keep things short and to the point, Natalie's older brother wouldn't stop butting in with questions about the game itself, until all the big plot details had been mentioned.

"Whoa..." Kyle was suitably impressed, at least. "Why can't my group's games do stuff like that?"

"Mixed blessing, kid." Uncle grimaced. "Interesting times, and all that. Still, I'd like to apologize. It should not have gotten as far as it did."

"How long's she been holed up in there?" asked Mr. Perkins with a sigh. The look on the man's face was not one of surprise at all, not even at the start of the long explanation.

"About twenty minutes now."

"Still well short of her record." The next sigh was louder. "I know how my daughter can get. She promised to be on her best behavior, but..."

"She got carried away, and things got out of hand," Uncle finished for him.

"Exactly."

At the table, the girls were all gathered around Helen. His niece was busy, her fingers flying as she sketched on some of his scrap paper. The others were holding sharpened pencils in a dozen colors, waiting to be of use. On the page, there was the picture of a girl, drawn to middle school standards with huge eyes and disproportionate head, and it only took a glance to tell who she was supposed to be. Black hair, tiara, golden armor with a sun-in-glory blazon: it was definitely Princess Isabel.

"Spelling check," he said, pointing to the words on a rough plan lying next to the main event. "Cœur is spelled C-O-E-U-R, with the O and the E joined at the hip 'cause it's French like that."

"Thanks," said Helen, fixing the word.

"So what's all this, then?" he asked.

He got a round table of guilty looks. "Well, um..." Helen began, "we were all sitting here and, um, got to feeling bad about how everything turned out..."

"Not that she didn't deserve it,"

317

harrumphed Shelby.

"...so we wanted to try and make it up to her somehow, and Katelyn suggested drawing a picture..."

"...yeah. Pictures are good."

"...and, well, Rob's your uncle, right?" Helen said with a grin.

Her own uncle, not named Rob, chuckled. "I think you mean 'Bob's your uncle.' Your mom's back to watching BBC programming again, I take it. Well, it's a nice idea, at least. Be sure to add a unicorn in the background," he suggested.

His niece nodded, and a few minutes later they had a rough portrait of Princess Isabel Cœur de Lion Solaire ready to present. The proportions were all wonky and the final coloring had been done by committee, but it wasn't half bad. Helen placed it inside a clear file and carefully slid it under the door of the girls' restroom.

A moment later, the lock clicked and Natalie stepped out with art in hand. Her eyes were still puffy and her nose was still runny, but the sobbing had stopped. She sniffled a bit as she looked at the other girls, but it was the sight of Claire that triggered the waterworks again.

"I'm sorry!" She was half a head taller than her cousin, obvious now that she had Claire in a huglock. The bespectacled little girl was squirming from the crush. "I'm so so so so so so so..."

"She gets the point," said Uncle. "Also, she needs to breathe."

"SORRY!" Natalie relaxed her grip. "I was silly and selfish and I ruined everyone's day again, and..." She had to pause for a breath herself.

"Can't say it wasn't interesting..." Cynthia ventured diplomatically. Around the circle, the other girls mumbled various sorts of vague agreement. Natalie brightened a little at the reassurances, meager as they were.

Uncle walked the Perkinses out to the parking lot. "Dunno if she'd want to," he said softly to her father, "and dunno how well it would turn out, but Natalie's welcome to come back anytime."

"We'll see." Mr. Perkins sighed again. It seemed to be a regular facet of his character. "I hope she at least learned something from this."

"I think they all did," said Uncle, pointedly not looking at the broad window of Max's Pizza, where five girls were watching their steps. "Offer still stands."

"Thank you." And with that, the Perkins family station wagon was off.

It was quiet at the table when he came back inside. "Well," he said. "Are we on for next week?" After a session like today's, he wouldn't have blamed anyone for wanting a break. Instead, he got a ragged chorus of "Yeah" which, while a little downhearted, was still an affirmative.

"Okay." He thought for a moment. "We'll pick up right from this point, next week. Only Selvi really got enough experience to go up a level from this fiasco, so this should give everyone a chance to catch up before the next big part. Claire, your princess will need to officially gain a level before she can commit to her new bunny-girl status, so no more transformation shenanigans before then. Capisce?"

"Comprendo, tío de los juegos!"

"Sorry, I took French in high school." He waited till the girls stopped giggling. Anyhoo, whether or not Natalie is back next week – and odds are that she won't be – you all get to drag Isabel through the next adventure as well. So, to give you something to think about..."

Dawn was just kissing the horizon when they arrived at the house of hospitality. Or rather, Gwen amended in her head, where Cassie said that Isabel had said she remembered such a house being on an old map back at her temple in Nordiv. Nothing about the place looked remotely hospitable. In the pre-dawn light, everything was a uniform grey, but even so it was obvious that the old manor before them was naturally a shade of dark charcoal. One wing of the building appeared to be in the middle of a collapse, and half of the visible windows were broken.

"What do you think?" she asked Selvi.

"Gotta rest somewhere, take this stupid load off," Selvi replied. The barbarian had the former paladin strapped to the back of her saddle, and was none too happy about it. "Not like we got much sleep tonight, and the sky's lookin' like rain later today. A broken roof's better'n none at all."

"There's a light on," Flora pointed out from atop Isabel's horse.

So there was, by a side door that had most likely been a servants' entrance. The stables were in decent shape, and the horses were happy enough in them. A quiet, mousy young woman answered the door, and soon they were shown to a small room with sleeping pallets for them all. After such a night, none of them put up much protest as sleep took them.

Uncle finished writing his notes for the next session. With all the girls already departed, he was free to pull out all of his resources without danger of tipping them off. He chuckled to himself as he leafed through a couple of handy source books. The next Sunday was going to be wicked.

Unseen and unheard by any of the princesses, the mousy young woman locked the door to the guest room behind her and hurried up a narrow set of stairs. Only one room on the third floor was occupied, or even furnished with anything more than vague, sheet-covered outlines of chairs and tables. In this room, everything was in pristine condition, with nary a mote of dust to mar the surface of the table wax.

With a curtsy, she made her report: "Guests, madam. Six. Tired. In the sleeping room."

"Thank you, dear child." The room's sole occupant turned from her writing desk to stroke the girl's cheek, like a beloved pet. "The sun is almost upon us, so let them sleep the day away." Now a sharp grin showed upon delicate white skin. "They shall be more entertaining when well rested."

Author's Note

Like so many things in life, this story started as a random thought at a random time, namely "What would happen if I got press-ganged into running a game for my niece and her hypothetical friends, because no one else knew what to do?" This was the result.

But I wanted to do it right, or at least right-ish. The actual game the girls are playing is a mish-mash of rules from things like Dungeons & Dragons and Pathfinder, with a very large helping of homebrewed imagination. It's sad to say, but dire were-rabbits are not a normal part of the gaming experience unless you add them in yourself.

Any time there's a dice roll mentioned in the story, there were actual plastic polyhedrons tumbling across a table, desk, tatami mat, whatever. This was especially crazy with Princess Bianca's magic rod, since it used a 100-sided die roll with around twenty different outcomes. Some times, the roll I really wanted to happen never did, like how I had actually planned out what to do if she rolled 36 (summon woolly rhinoceros) in Episode 2. The roll was 39 (lightning bolt), so I never got to use it, unfortunately. He was going to be Gwen's animal companion. The girls were going to name him something mundanely silly like Larry. *C'est la vie.*

That's certainly been half the fun of this project, however, that I've given a significant amount of leeway to the planning stages just because dice rolls can throw things in odd directions. It's been a blast, and I hope others can enjoy reading these stories as much as I've enjoyed writing them.

All three episodes in this volume were originally sold as e-books on Amazon Kindle, and the fourth episode, *Grandmothers and Other Fearsome Encounters*, is already available there as well. The fifth episode, *Boyfriends and Other Minor Annoyances*, should be out by March 2018.

Thanks for reading!

Made in the USA
Middletown, DE
18 July 2018